TANTALIZER VOL. 1:

JUST THE TIP

Copyright © 2024 Hedone Books

All rights reserved.

The characters and events portrayed in this book are fictitious. Any similarity to real persons, living or dead, is coincidental and not intended by the authors.

No part of this book may be reproduced, or stored in a retrieval system, or transmitted in any form or by any means, electronic, mechanical, photocopying, recording, or otherwise, without express written permission of the publisher.

Cover design: Caitlin Marceau
Edited by: Evelyn Freeling, Marina Garrido, Caitlin Marceau, Nelka Mazur

CONTENTS

A LETTER FROM THE EDITORS

THANK YOU ALL FOR TAKING THE TIME TO GRAB A COPY OF Hedone Books' *Tantalizer Vol. 1: Just The Tip*. While we hope this collection of short stories, interviews, submission calls, and excerpts leaves you satisfied, we also hope it has you *begging* for more. (What can we say? We love edging.)

At Hedone, one of our goals is to showcase the many forms that erotic horror can take. From the explicitly devious, like Lindz McLeod's "Natural Disaster" or Dori Lumpkin's "Don't Hang Up The Phone," to the dark and sensual, like S. M. Hallow's *How To Survive This Fairytale* and Antonia Rachel Ward's *Ondine's Curse*, we firmly believe that there's something for everyone when it comes to erotic horror. Different strokes for different folks, as all the horny readers would say.

In addition to providing a variety of content, we aim to give readers a safe place to experiment with kink, explore their sexuality, and test their boundaries. There's a significant lack of queer content, marginalized voices, and diversity when it comes to horror-otica and dark romance. It's a gaping hole in the publishing industry that we can't wait to fill.

There's terror in desire. It forces us to question who we are, what we want, and why.

While we might not have the answers for you here and now, we do hope that you'll find them in the pages of one of our books.

As long as it's not this one.

It is *Just The Tip*, afterall.

Sincerely,

The Hedone Books Editorial Team

ps. Make sure to scan the Spotify barcodes throughout this book. Each one leads to a curated playlist from each story's author!

MEET THE TEAM

NELKA MAZUR (THEY/THEM/SHE/HER)

NELKA MAZUR IS A QUEER BOOK REVIEWER AND EDITOR hailing from New England. Their passion for horror grew from being raised inside a movie rental store, gazing at VHS covers, and never looking back. They've worked with Women in Horror, sponsored and judged submissions for the Ax Wound Film Festival, and actively discusses books and advocates for the horror genre on social media under @CozyGinger.

TURN ONS:

Cannibalism as a love language. Body horror representing true self. Medical horror as foreplay. Queer relationship dynamics with a focus on sapphic relationships. Underrepresented relationship pairings. Fever dream inner dialogue. Unhinged, passionate, and violent main characters. Vivid, well-described, visceral gore. Taboo kinks and sex play. Pushing boundaries while breaking industry norms about sex and identity. Irredeemable main characters with no redemption arc. Characters that are over thirty. Anything and everything cosmic.

TURN OFFS:

I especially hate traditional contemporary love dialogue. Thinly veiled rape fantasies and violence against femmes steeped in misogyny. Barely legal main characters. Poorly written gross-out scenes just to be gross. Love interests and/or sex partners with little to no humanoid resemblance. Miscommunication. Pregnancy as an ending. Extreme angst.

HARD NOS:

Beastiality, pedophilia, work promoting hate.

KINKS:

- *Waif* by Samantha Kolesnik
- *The Ecstasy of Agony* by Wrath James White
- *Claustrophilia* by Ezra Blake
- *Deliver Me* by Elle Nash

- *The Unbeating Heart* by Cyran Faringray
- *Girl Flesh* by May Leitz
- *The Skeleton King* by Charity B.
- *Exquisite Corpse* by Poppy Z. Brite
- *In The Miso Soup* by Ryu Murakami
- *Heartless Heathens* by Santana Knox
- The Hellraiser franchise
- Cut a hole and fuck it.

CAITLIN MARCEAU (SHE/HER/THEY/THEM)

Caitlin Marceau is a queer Canadian author and illustrator known for her award-winning novella *This Is Where We Talk Things Out*. Her forthcoming work includes *It Wasn't Supposed To Go Like This*, *I'm Having Regrets*, and the sequel to her debut novella, *All Roads Lead Us Home*. For more, find her on social media with the handle @Caitlin-Marceau or check out her website at CaitlinMarceau.ca.

TURN ONS:

Genres and conventions I love include eco-eroticism, good-for-her narratives, folk horror, women's wrongs, body horror dripping with

Gothic elements, dark academia, bleak urban fantasies, and unhappy endings. I'm especially interested in stories that include marginalized bodies, queer characters, non-Western narratives, unconventional relationships, and work that decentres heteronormativity. I'm also interested in stories that include femme dommes and masc subs, reverse and/or gender diverse harems, BDSM (with emphasis on S/M dynamics), vore, edging, enemies to lovers or lovers to enemies, taboo relationship dynamics, kink, paranormal erotica, religion (with an emphasis on ritual and/or the aesthetics of Catholicism) and/or religious trauma. Although I'm open to reading work with comedic elements, the piece itself shouldn't be outright comedy.

TURN OFFS:

Tender romances without conflict or eroticism, stereotypical relationships, flat characters, fetishizing marginalization, manic pixie dream girls, cultural appropriation, consensual non-consent (CNC), furries, monsters that closely resemble real animals, stories that center on comphet and/or cishet relationships, pregnancy.

HARD NOS:

Bestiality, incest, pedophilia, rape, works promoting hate.

KINKS:

- *Jennifer's Body* (Karyn Kusama, 2009)
- *The VVitch* (Robert Eggers, 2015)
- *Suspiria* (Luca Guadagnino, 2018)
- *Antiviral* (Brandon Cronenberg, 2012)
- *Last Night In Soho* (Edgar Wright, 2021)
- *Midsommar* (Ari Aster, 2019)
- *Titane* (Julia Ducourneau, 2021)

- *Merciless Waters* by Rae Wilde
- *To Be Devoured* by Sara Tantlinger
- *Marionette* by Antonia Rachel Ward
- Anything and everything by Kelley Armstrong

Lindz McLeod

NATURAL DISASTER

NATURAL DISASTER

I STARTED MASTURBATING TO NATURAL DISASTERS WHEN I WAS sixteen. Not the aftermath, obviously; dead people did nothing for me. Bloated corpses floating amongst shattered houses, crushed limbs under dusty, grey rubble, lifeless limpets spread out on plastic sheets—I'd watched the newsreels just like everyone else, and they hadn't given me so much as a pussy twinge.

No, I'd decided, it was the anticipation of the act itself which turned me on. The moment before the tsunami hit, like a hand slicing through air to land on an upturned bare ass. The rumbling twinges of earth that preceded the actual orgasm of rupture. The volcano—self-explanatory. Some people liked to be teased, to have their bodies barely touched, while some people only fucked to finish. Personally, I liked how it felt midway through. The swelling, the rising, the simmer.

The Goldilocks of sex, neither too cold nor too hot.

While Mattie was fucking me, I was thinking about his hot new roommate, Lena, and how her hair and her eyebrows were an unnatural pale, almost white, and how it kind of made me want to dress up as a furry to see if I could convince her to play wolf-eating-the-grandmother, and—

Mid thrust, Mattie squeezed his eyes shut and gasped, "Yeah! Yeah! I'm going to be a Sunbather!"

"What the fuck?" I said, and pushed him off.

"I mean," he shrugged, cheeks flushed, "obviously."

I didn't think it was obvious at all. "Don't most people die trying?"

"Come on, Roz," he wheedled, "let me finish before we have a philosophical debate."

I thought about saying no, but I had been close too. I lay back, running my hands across my pale thighs, my flat stomach, my freckled chest, watching his pupils dilate and his cock twitch. His hands, stubby-fingered with square nails—spade hands, good for digging deep—clamped onto my hips.

"Longer thrusts," I instructed him, and pulled his hair until he complied, squealing.

Afterwards, he lit a joint, took a deep pull before passing it over. "Don't you think they're awesome?"

"Not really." The weed was smoother than usual, with a berry-flavored afterburn. "Seems like a huge risk."

He grinned. "I eat risk for breakfast."

"You eat Pop Tarts," I corrected him and, predictably distracted, he spent the next five minutes regaling me with his usual indignant lecture on why the frosted cinnamon apple jack tart au pop was the most superior breakfast item ever made.

I WASN'T EXPECTING HIM TO ACTUALLY GO THROUGH WITH IT. I mean, sure, I'd seen the Sunbathers on TV—we all had—but Mattie wasn't the most colorful crayon in the packet. The kind of guy who's either welded to his couch or his skateboard, and in between he's baked as fuck or jittering from room to room, twanging guitars and quoting out-of-context lines from Christopher Nolan films.

I'd started my seduction of Lena early, coming around before Mattie had got home from whatever shitty job he'd scrounged this week, or lingering long after he'd left for a shift. The Swede was on some kind of work-abroad scheme with one of the local corporations, focusing on climate change. She told me about dams breaking, about atmospheric rivers hovering above us just waiting to hammer us with a deluge that would make Noah's flood look positively tame. Christ, it made me wet.

"I love your hair," I said, leaning over to touch a loose strand. "Is your whole family this blonde? Wow, it's so soft."

"Oh, thank you. I use a special—" She frowned, staring over my shoulder. "Is— Is that Matthew?"

I turned, following her gaze. On TV, a group of bright-pink and shiny-black people milled around like puppies. At the forefront, a man with a puffed chest and impossibly bright teeth smiled up at the shaky camera. It was Mattie, bright and bold and glorious. His shoulders were bullish, solid. His perfect pecs rippled above a stark eight pack. His thighs were quivering, golden flanks; they could have ploughed fields.

Frankly, he'd never looked so unfuckable.

"Oh god, he really did it." Irritation vied with admiration. I really hadn't expected him to live through the Burn, which required one to stay outside during one of the big solar flares. Most people baked to death, while those who lived turned into basically reverse-vampires, becoming impervious to the sun's deadly glare and weak to the dark of night. What little research there had been into what qualified a person for Sunbather-hood was vague and ambiguous. It seemed like the sun had its own conditions regarding what it considered worthy, and whatever those might be, no one could guess.

I FOUND MATTIE THE NEXT DAY, LOOKING TANNED RATHER than pink, lingering outside his old apartment block. His hair was different—a sunblushed, honeyed chestnut instead of the usual tree-bark grey-brown. Even his dick was bigger, meatier. Up close, my first impression solidified. I'd never been into gym rats; they were too basic, too boring.

"Hi," he said, grinning as if expecting me to open my legs right there and then, reaching down to tug at his cock. "Come here."

I watched from the comfort of the building's shade. I tanned okay, but it was midmorning, and the heat was starting to prickle uncomfortably. "Nah."

"What do you mean, nah?" He looked down at his perfect body, opened his arms wide. "I'm a god now, Roz. You always wanted to fuck a god, right?"

I pushed my tongue into my cheek, vaguely recalling I'd said something of the sort months ago. Trust Mattie to take everything seriously, to commit all my words to memory and try to use them to nail me in every sense of the word. "I meant like an old god. Lovecraftian. Tentacles and hundreds of teeth and shit like that. You look like Ski Bunny Ken wished hard enough to become a real boy." I rolled my eyes. "Western masculinity at its finest. Congratulations."

Even under his tan, I could see an angry flush spread up his neck. "You could be a Sunbather too, you know." His voice was cool, but not quite steady.

"You're kidding, right?"

"We're the future," he insisted. "And we could be together, like, forever."

"Is that what you thought this was?" Laughing was a bad idea, but I couldn't help myself. "I thought gods were above monogamy."

A muscle in his jaw jumped. "You'll come around, Roz," he promised. "You'll see. You just don't know what you're missing. I've never felt so amazing."

"Yeah, well, good luck with that." He opened his mouth to speak again, but I slid through the door of the apartment building and closed it in his face. He sounded a lot like he was on coke, which I'd tried twice and hated both times; having that much self-assurance was unnatural. The thing that made me walk a high wire with so much confidence was knowing just how far I could fall if everything went wrong. A heady cocktail of homegrown arrogance, lust, and vodka usually worked fine for me, and I saw no reason to change that now.

MATTIE HUNG AROUND THE APARTMENTS DURING THE DAY, waiting to accost me on my way to work. He tried every tactic he could think of—wheedling, negging, flattering, appealing to a sense of religiosity he knew I didn't possess, shaming, guilt-tripping—but every word out of his mouth turned me off more and more. Eventually, his words had taken on an aggressive edge, and when he'd grabbed me, I'd screamed bloody murder. Shaken, he'd backed off long enough for me to escape into the confines of Riverside Plaza, but I'd vowed not to walk during the day any more, at least until his stupid obsession had waned. My boss, after seeing a huge blue bruise erupt on my forearm, encouraged me to work from home.

After the sun had set that evening, I wandered back to Mattie's apartment, where Lena was delighted to see me. With Mattie gone all night, she was home alone and very clearly on edge. It took three nights of sharing takeout, plying her with vodka, letting her teach me some pretty-sounding Swedish, and painting my nails a truly garish shade of orange, before recognition dawned in her eyes. I saw it, and she knew I saw it, and I let her stuttering refusal fade into silence—her mouth a door, half-wedged between desire and fear—before I leaned forward and kissed her. A few minutes of making out had her pressing me up against the door, rutting like some half-crazed buck. Her small bedroom was smoggy with incense, her bedsheets crisp and cool. Undressed, Lena looked like the kind of pale fish that lived under a rock, like a Scandinavian river ghost waiting to drown errant travelers.

I'd never been wetter in my life.

Her fingers fumbled at my clit, stuttered at my hole before sliding in. I clenched around the bony dice of her knuckles, moaned at the joy of finally being filled. Above her bed, a crucifix hung. Eighteen-ab

Jesus stared down at us, his gaunt cheeks hollowed with unspeakable suffering. I came staring at his dick-ribboned crotch.

I didn't waste time catching my breath before I returned the favour. Her milky thighs clamped around my skull the moment my tongue touched quivering pink flesh, and I had the distinct and bizarre mental image of a series of planets crashing into each other, like a real-life Newton's Cradle. Settling into broad strokes, punctuated by occasional narrow circles, I ate her pussy like I was condemned and she was my last meal. Timing my licks with her rising shrieks, I applied a little pressure against her asshole with my pinkie, just enough to tickle the sensitive nerves there, and felt her orgasm crash upwards with all the grinding certainty of a tectonic plate.

I waited until she'd fallen asleep, clinging to me like a treasured teddy bear, before slipping out and strolling back to my own apartment. I lived only three blocks away, and the night air was refreshing, the moon a pallid, pregnant gibbous. No Sunbather could touch me at this hour, so all I had to watch out for were the usual human problems, though there seemed like far less of them than usual. The streets were near silent, no drunken yodeling from the nearby karaoke bar, and the few people I did see scuttled quickly into the shadows.

I texted Lena the next morning and when she didn't reply, I assumed she was either already busy or regretted our fling, or both. After all, despite my insistence that Mattie and I were no more than a casual thing, clearly he hadn't seen it that way. I had no way of knowing what lovelorn pronouncements he'd made in private over the last few months. I shrugged, and applied myself to my own work, editing legal contracts for a large architectural firm. Ursula the sea witch had been a big childhood inspiration of mine; in my view, she'd done nothing wrong and in fact had highlighted the negative aspects of the T's and C's of the contract between herself and Ariel much more clearly than any regular human lawyer would have bothered to do for a client they were planning on screwing over. It wasn't exactly a dream job, but it was soothing in a repetitive way, and it more than paid my modest bills.

The text came later, mid-afternoon. *Would you like to see me again?* Oddly formal, but sure, why not. *Yeah*, I replied. *When?*

Now? she suggested.

I'm not sure, I texted. She'd seen the bruise, she'd known what Mattie had done, what he'd become.

Now? she said again.

I frowned. That sounded more like a call for help. Or a trap. I turned my phone face down and kept working. When I checked a couple of hours later, there were no new messages. I waited until the sun had set before going back to to her apartment Lena wasn't there. I buzzed several times, but no one came to the door. Standing across the street, I squinted up at the second floor window, but the place lay in darkness.

He'd convinced her to turn, I was certain of it. Fucking idiot. Not that I'd known her well, so it was possible that she might have survived the Burn, but the odds weren't great. It was so like Mattie to do something stupid and drag other people along on his harebrained scheme. Returning home, I slid into bed after a quick, cool shower, my eyes itching from all the screen-time, my body buzzing with pent up energy. I pictured them standing in the plaza at noon, naked and golden, kissing like movie stars—all movement, no passion. Pictured him laying her on the crispy grass, her eyes comically wide open to stop from imagining me in place of Mattie, my knowing fingers skating in place of his predictable too-hard button-mashing. Pictured watching them fuck through a gap in the trees, my hand slapping against my underwear, enjoying the feeling of being chained by cotton, of not quite getting enough reach. Paused my view mid-frame, stopped his taut, grilled-tan ass plummeting downwards with every thrust, drew every grunt and shrill moan downwards into low bass, like a slowed-down record. I wanted to find their deepest wounds and stick my fingers in every raw, aching hole. Maybe gouge some new ones, too.

Biting down onto my bruised arm I rose off the bed with an orgasm as sudden and sharp as a thunderclap, and flopped back bonelessly against the now-sweaty sheets. Sucking my fingers clean, I drifted off into a contented sleep. Whatever the outcome, neither of them were my problem any more.

THE SUNBATHERS BECOME MORE PREVALENT. NOT A SINGLE day went by without several news articles about them: their preaching, their certainty, their growing numbers which had begun to raise concerns among the authorities. The danger had always been apparent to me; a packed go-bag had lain on the floor of my closet for two months, and lately I'd taken to opening the door and simply staring at it for a while.

As the Sunbathers became more violent, I took more notice. Their perfection had turned me off before, but the sheer ferocity, uncaged, began to turn me on in a different way. Watching them beat on a crowd of football fans—tossing 300-pound guys aside like ragdolls, tearing the stadium seats out, bending the goalposts with their bare hands—made my cunt twitch. Something about them got me hot and bothered just like natural disasters did. A hurricane wrenching up a roof just to dump it three miles west. A plague of locusts, eating up everything in their path. That endless hunger, that yawning, desperate need to ravage and ruin for savagery's own sake. I understood it only too well. There was something about the world going wrong that made me feel so, so right.

Late one afternoon, I chanced a quick trip to the grocery store. I was sick of scavenging from what was left once the sun went down, and besides, I was out of my favourite quadruple-chocolate cookies, to say nothing of my depleted stores of vodka. To my chagrin, the nearest store was sold out of both, but my craving had already set in. Cursing under my breath, I skulked through the back alleys, a grimy baseball cap pulled low over my face. Though I stuck to the shadows as much as possible, occasional glints of sun seared my cheeks and exposed hands. I'd put sunblock on, of course, but even the highest factors were all but useless these days.

The next grocery store was two blocks past my old office building at Riverside Plaza, and thankfully had a few packets of cookies left. I bought every single one with petty relish, as well as four litres of vodka. My backpack weighed a ton but it was better to have both hands free, just in case shit went down. On the return journey, a shriek of pain shook me from my thoughts. I halted, hesitated, wondering whether to double back and cut down another street, but curiosity got the better of me. I inched towards the corner of the nearest building and peered around it.

A man and a woman stood over a prone, groaning figure. Naked. Very clearly a Sunbather. *Shit.* I bit back a gasp—how the hell had they managed to capture one? A dribble of blood from his temple provided a single clue, but even at this late hour, surely a Sunbather would have been able to overpower two puny, regular people. I sidled around the corner, careful to stick to the shadows, and stood directly under the CCTV, out of the line of sight. I recognized the humans from Riverside—he was a security guard, still dressed in his blue uniform shirt and pants, while she was one of the upper floor account managers, her her tight white blouse straining as she leaned over and spat onto the Sunbather's face.

The captive turned his head away, and I caught a glimpse of strange handcuffs—not the slender usual kind that assisted cops or bondage, but thick, padded ones. I expected to see them glowing or crackling but they were disappointingly normal. How were they keeping a Sunbather in check? And how long would it last? The sky was already fading into a brilliant orange, and the Sunbather was in visible distress. I leaned against the wall, excited to see the horror show play out, my cunt twitching in anticipation. I hadn't been laid in two weeks, and the atmosphere was thick with the feeling of disaster.

The security guard booted the Sunbather right in the dick. "That's for my sister, you fucking asshole."

Ah, so it's personal, I thought. *Not just a performance to show what we're capable of.* The account manager stared up at the sky. "Not long now."

"You're... you're making a huge mistake," the Sunbather croaked, turning his head back. His eyes were big and black, the pupils blown out of all proportion. Even from twenty feet away, I could see the veins in his neck pulsing. "We endured the heat to walk in light. You have no right to take that from me."

"You think you're so much better than us, don't you?" the account manager sneered. "But you're not. You promise people glory, then laugh when they burn. Fucking monster. Fucking inhuman *thing*."

The sun dipped behind a building, the shadows lengthening. "Grace?" the security guard said, and the account manager took his hand as the Sunbather began to scream, his golden skin burnishing to a luminous, glacial gleam, like a negative of a photograph. I blinked, thinking it must be a trick of the light, but no, he was gurgling, something white running from his eyes and ears and mouth and dick and ass, pooling under his body in a large, milky puddle. After long moments, it was all over and he lay still, his twitches slowing to a standstill.

"Is he dead?" the security guard asked, his voice shaky. "Did we kill him?"

The account manager prodded the body. "I think so." She She smirked. "Whoops. Oh well."

I couldn't help snorting. She glanced over her shoulder at me, her smirk growing, then unbuttoned her blouse. The security guard tore at his own shirt, ripping it open. They pawed frantically at each other, before dropping to their knees. The account manager bent over the Sunbather's body, dipping her hand into the white pool of whatever it was, and reached back, coating the guard's swollen cock. They fucked on top of the corpse as if the Sunbather was a low table, using the weight to brace themselves. Smears of white leaked down the manager's thighs, pooling on the Sunbather's motionless, toned stomach. I should have called out to ask them what the handcuffs did; maybe if I had, things would have worked out differently later. Instead, I yanked my jeans down to mid-thigh and, biting my lip, went to town, working my clit to the steady thwap-thwap rhythm they'd set. When I'd finished, I left them to their machinations, still resolutely pounding away, their mouths agape, faces twisted in the kind of pleasure-pain that can only come from doing something you know you'll regret later.

The Sunbathers came after those people, of course, once they realised what had happened. They tore the windows off the lobby of Riverside Plaza and dragged out the security guard and all his security guard buddies. They came back the next day and smashed in all the windows. Murdered the executives, tore apart the account managers, rooted out the admin workers in their little cubicles. Some people now refer to this as the start of the war, the single action that precipitated all the terrible things that came afterwards. Others have described time as a tree; history is merely the roots, each feeding into a thick present trunk, branching off into the slender twigs of our potential futures. Still, it's clear that something was sparked that day. The Sunbathers were never going to take kindly to someone killing one of their own, to blot out the great sacrifice and gracious benevolence of one of the sun's representatives on Earth. Any fool could see that.

By the time dawn rose the next morning, I was long gone.

LINDZ MCLEOD

"SUNBATHERS"

Sin is hot, but purity is blistering. *Hordes of cannibalistic sun vampires rule the day, forcing humans to hide at night. Soph is bored with her grubby, nocturnal existence. When she sacrifices everything to become a Sunbather, she discovers the heterosexual commune is not the glowing paradise she'd hoped for and her new, immortal body still desires womanflesh. As the Sunbathers construct a lamp that will enable them to walk in light at all times of day, Soph must decide if she's willing to doom what's left of humanity to finally fit in.*

Lindz McLeod is a queer, working-class, Scottish writer and poet who dabbles in the surreal. Her short prose has been published by *Apex*, *Catapult*, *Pseudopod*, and many more. Her longer work includes the short story collection *Turducken* (Spaceboy, 2023), as well as her novels *Beast* (Hear Us Scream, 2023), *Sunbathers* (Hedone Books, 2024), *The Unlikely Pursuit Of Mary Bennet* (Harlequin, 2025), and *An Honour And A Privilege* (Stanchion, 2025). Her work has been taught in schools, universities, and turned into avant-garde opera. She is a full member of the SFWA, the club president of the Edinburgh Writers' Club, and is currently studying for a PhD in Creative Writing.

HOW TO SURVIVE THIS FAIRYTALE

S. M. HALLOW

. Kill Snow White. Kill Snow White. Kill Sn

. Kill Snow White. Kill Snow White. Kill Sn

w White. Kill Snow White. Kill Snow White

. Kill Snow White. Kill Snow White. Kill Sn

hite. Kill Snow White. Kill Snow White. Kil

KILL SNOW WHITE

ITE. KILL SNOW KILL SNOW

HOW TO SURVIVE THIS FAIRYTALE

A PROLOGUE:

A FATHER LEADS HIS CHILDREN INTO THE WOODS AND LEAVES them there.

1. FIRST, YOU HAVE TO WANT TO LIVE.

Which you do, more than anything else. Why else the pebbles? Why else the bread crumbs?

Here's the thing: you can lie down and die at any time. When you and your sister are abandoned to the woods, with no way home, and no one at home who wants you, you can surrender and sink into the sleep that has no end.

But you don't.

No: you take your sister's hand, and you wander through the labyrinthine wood until your feet blister and your bearings blur. Even then, you're not ready to die.

And when the wolf comes?

When the wolf comes–its fur drawn tight over visible ribs that mirror your own withered body–you can submit to the mercy of its slavering maw. You and your sister. You can let it end for the both of you, but you don't.

Instead, you take your sister's hand, and you run.

Even though you can't outrun a wolf, even though the low-hanging branches of the trees snatch at your shoulders, even though you've soiled yourself in fear and Gretel's tears flow endlessly.

Despite it all, you keep running.

Why?

Why keep running?

Why resist, when the ending seems inevitable?

Why eat of the house made of spun sugar and ginger cake?

Because you have one glorious, wretched life, and, for whatever reason, you'll hold onto it until giants grind your bones to make their bread.

Remember this when it gets harder.

Because it only gets harder from here.

2. IF YOU WANT TO LIVE, YOU HAVE TO BE CLEVER.

You traded one danger for another: a wolf for a witch.

You couldn't have known the house was a trap.

Now you do.

Locked in a child-sized cage in a corner of the witch's kitchen, you know so much more about this world than you're ready to know. The witch has you where she wants you, and if you want to avoid joining the bones that litter the bottom of your cage, you're going to have to *think*.

Your only idea is to refuse the meals Gretel brings you. You try with all your might to resist each warm loaf of bread, each sliced apple served with nuts, each hunk of meat...

... and even though you know the witch is fattening you up for the table...

... even though you know you should be wary of the meat...

... you tumble mouth-first into each plate, entranced.

"Hansel, don't," Gretel whispers in the dark, her voice thin and shaking. "Don't eat it. Every bite only makes you want more."

But you can't hear her. Not really.

"There's enough for us to share," you say, and offer her a spoonful of rich, hearty stew. "We've never had food like this in our lives. Not ever."

She refuses you three times a day, every day, for a week.

And then the witch comes.

"Let us see if you're ready," she says. "Put a finger through the cage, boy."

(*A finger? Why a finger?* Stop it. Don't ask questions. The story needn't make sense. This is simply how the story goes.)

You've had seven days to prepare for this. Seven days to shake off the haze of her bounty and think of a way out. You haven't thought of a way out. You've thought only of your full belly—*full*, for the first time in years—and when your next meal will arrive. What a strange thing, to be full and yet keep yearning for more. You hadn't thought it strange until just this moment. You hadn't given yourself time to think of anything but *food*, and its endless, abundant, reliable delivery.

Frigid realization sloshes through you. You were supposed to think of a way out, and you didn't. You want to live and you're not going to live.

You offer the witch your finger. She gropes it and cackles.

"Gretel, *darling*," she sneers, "prepare the cauldron."

THAT CAN'T BE THE WAY THIS STORY ENDS.

TRY AGAIN?

"Let us see if you're ready," says the witch. "Put a finger through the cage, boy."

You've had seven days to prepare for this, but the idea doesn't strike you until the last possible moment.

Instead of offering the witch your finger, you stick a bone through the bars of your cage. You're sorry for the children who've died before you, but grateful for them, too. All of them, and the one in particular whose bone you're using to save your own life.

"*What?* How can this be?" the witch bellows. Her sightless eyes narrow. Her anger pulses through her with such strength you expect she'll puff steam. Then she composes herself.

"You must have been skinnier than I thought," she says, "if a week of good meals won't stick to your bones. Very well, very well... Another week."

ANOTHER, AND ANOTHER, AND ANOTHER. FOUR WEEKS PASS, and you've done little more than buy yourself time.

"I've been eating the house," Gretel whispers. "It's different than the food she gives you."

"Different how?" you ask.

"It's... changing me."

"Changing you?"

The floorboards creak. Gretel's eyes widen and she shakes her head. Maybe in another story, you convince her to tell you more, but in this one? In this one, she collects your empty dishes—each plate licked clean for the very last crumbs—and disappears.

"I'VE WAITED LONG ENOUGH," SAYS THE WITCH. "SKINNY OR fat, I eat the boy today. Gretel, turn on the oven."

A horrible silence.

"But... last time you wanted your cauldron," says Gretel. She risks a glance at you. Somehow you sense that a plan to save you has just gone awry.

"Last time I wanted to boil him in a stew," says the witch. "Now I want to bake him into a pie."

Another, more horrible silence.

"A pie?"

Gretel's stalling.

"Don't just stand there," the witch barks, "turn on the oven!"

"But Grandmother," says Gretel, "I don't know how."

"You don't know *how*?"

The witch cannot see, yet she sees right through that lie. She snatches Gretel by the roots of her hair, opens the oven door, and shoves her inside. Like a Venus flytrap, the oven door snaps shut. Your little sister screams, but there's nothing you can do.

"Don't worry, boy," she says. "You'll join her soon."

THAT CAN'T BE THE WAY THIS STORY ENDS.

TRY AGAIN?

"Don't just stand there," the witch barks, "turn on the oven!"

"But Grandmother," says Gretel, "I don't know how."

"You don't know *how*?"

Remember: if you want to live, you have to be clever.

"It's true," you offer, before the witch can scent the lie in the air. "Our mother died when we were young, so we never learned how."

"Useless children," she hisses. "No wonder you were left in the woods."

The witch opens the oven door, and then: chaos.

Gretel on the witch's back. Gretel pulling the witch's silver hair. The witch clawing open Gretel's calves. The witch's teeth sharpening into fangs. Both of them shouting—Gretel's high-pitched scream, the witch's lowing growl. The witch bucking like a wild horse, and Gretel's hands in her mane of cobwebs, hanging on.

The bone that has saved you for a month saves you again as you use it to pick the lock of your cage.

The cage bursts open just as Gretel and the witch both tumble into the oven.

As soon as their bodies hit the metal rack within, the door slams shut.

Listen: some stories have endings before they begin. Your ending is already written in stone, and you won't make it there if you cannot follow instructions. Sometimes, it will seem like you have choices—this moment is one such illusion. Years from now, you will look back and wonder what you might have done differently. Rest assured, there was nothing. There is only one thing you can do: what you're told.

S. M. HALLOW

"HOW TO SURVIVE THIS FAIRYTALE"

At the mercy of a despotic narrator, Hansel must do as he's commanded to find his Happy Ending with his True Love or die, again and again. But when the narrator demands that he serve the evil queen and kill Snow White, Hansel decides to break free from his storyline. In this deconstruction of the fairy tales we all know and love, S. M. Hallow explores autonomy and learning self-forgiveness through love.

S. M. Hallow is a part-time fairytale witch, full-time vampire nominated for the Pushcart Prize, Best of the Net, and Best Microfiction. Hallow's stories, poems, and visual art can be found in *Baffling Magazine*, *Best of Fantasy Volume 3*, *CatsCast*, *Seize the Press*, and *Taco Bell Quarterly*, among others. To learn more, follow Hallow on Tumblr and Twitter at the handle @smhallow, and on Instagram with the username @smhallowink.

edited by

Lindz McLeod

Submission Call

MONSTER LOVERS VOL. 1: THE '80S

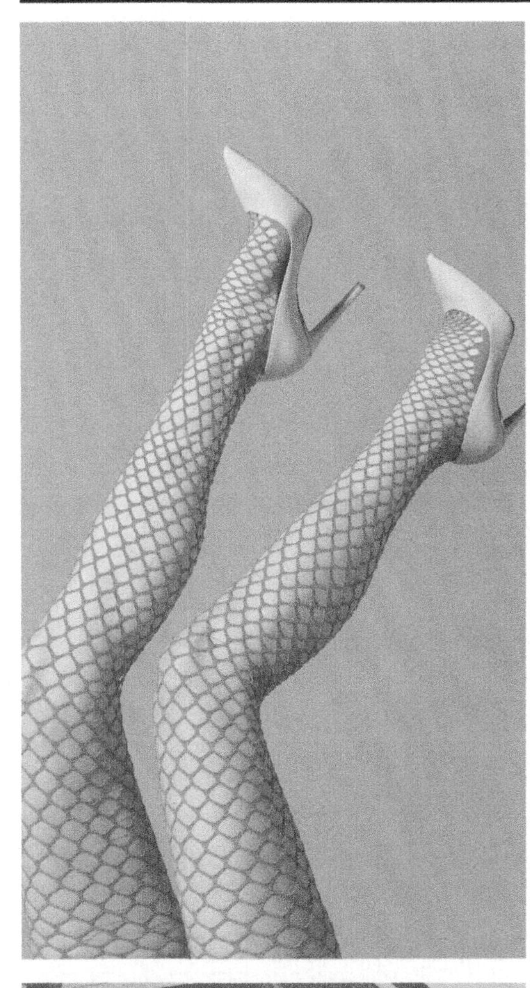

SUBMISSION CALL: "MONSTER LOVERS VOL. 1: THE '80S" EDITED BY LINDZ MCLEOD

THE '80S WERE A TIME OF GREAT CHANGE; GONE WERE THE placid browns and yellows and beiges of the '70s, and in their place swelled neon bright flowers and wild, individualistic styles embodied by fashion icons like Grace Jones and Madonna. With the rise of MTV, pop culture changed and expanded, and the course of mainstream culture was forever altered by the rivers of new music styles: punk, hip-hop, synth-pop. Despite this—and because of it—Reagan, Thatcher, and other world leaders argued for a moral citizenry who adhered to gender norms and strict heterosexuality, who dutifully bought into rampant capitalism and consumerism to fuel the government agendas.

We say: fuck all that.

Literally.

Stories submitted to *Monster Lovers Vol. 1: The '80s* should be set in that specific decade, though the location is entirely your own choice. Often blending horror with comedy (both intentionally and unintentionally), the '80s saw a return of old tropes like zombies and vampires now subverted in slick, satirical stories or presented as gory and over-the-top grotesqueness. We're inspired by Nancy A. Collins *Sunglasses*

After Dark, Stephen King's *Christine*, Dan Simmons' *Carrion Comfort*, and the stylings of the popular TV shows *Murder She Wrote*, *Miami Vice*, *Teenage Mutant Ninja Turtles*, and *Quantum Leap*. This editor is also extremely partial to *The Golden Girls*, and would love to see your take on this theme—not all monster lovers are athletic, bouffant twenty-year-olds, after all.

With this anthology, we're looking for stories from 2k to 5k words (firm) which explore '80s horror with a sexy or erotic spin. We're pledging that at least 70% of the submissions for this anthology come from unsolicited authors.

WHAT WE WOULD LOVE TO SEE: IN THIS ANTHOLOGY WE'RE looking for neon glow sticks in unexpected places, aerobics instructors in leg warmers getting thigh-fucked, rising up against the man in more ways than one. Show us sentient Rubik's Cubes with Tom Selleck mustaches, Thriller zombies getting handsy in movie theatres, back-combed Bowie-obsessed werewolves, vampires rocking to Def Leppard in skintight leather. Show us what else lurks in the shadows behind the club playing Whitney Houston's early hits. Show us a person stuck forever as a pencil drawing in the "Take On Me" video or what happens when you don't return your porn videos to Blockbusters on time. Show us sexy *Blade Runner* replicants finding new ways to pleasure each other, Beetlejuice as a ghoulish threesome, Poltergeist wielding sex toys, a squad of Ghostbusters proving that busting makes *everyone* feel good. Without using copyrighted material, such as character names, we invite you to explore the best and the worst that the '80s had to offer through an erotic lens.

WHAT WE DON'T WANT: RAPE FANTASIES, BESTIALITY, WORKS promoting hateful ideologies including homophobia and transphobia, and stories including sexual content with minors. Please note that for this call, we will not be accepting stories with consensual non-consent (CNC) in them.

SUBMISSION PERIOD: FEBRUARY 1, 2025 - MARCH 31, 2025

LENGTH: 2,000 - 5,000 WORDS

PAYMENT: $0.01 USD PER WORD

FORMAT: STORIES SHOULD BE FORMATTED IN 12 PT. TIMES New Roman, double spaced. Please include your pen name and author email address, but do not include your phone number or home address. Please include trigger warnings at the top of the page.

RIGHTS: EXCLUSIVE FIRST WORLDWIDE PUBLICATION, PRINT and Electronic Rights for one year (from date of publication), and non-exclusive rights thereafter.

CONTRIBUTOR COPIES: ONE PHYSICAL COPY AND ONE DIGITAL copy.

SIMULTANEOUS SUBMISSIONS: ALLOWED, BUT PLEASE promptly withdraw your story if it is accepted elsewhere. No reprints or multiple submissions.

CONTACT: ALL SUBMISSIONS SHOULD BE SENT TO submissions@hedonebooks.com. (Word files only, please do not paste your story in the body of the email.) The subject line of your email should read: MONSTER LOVERS VOL.1: THE '80S — "Story Title" — Author Name — Word Count

Responses: We aim to finalize the table of contents for the first issue by May 1, 2025.

FORGIVE ME, FATHER

Ashley Michele

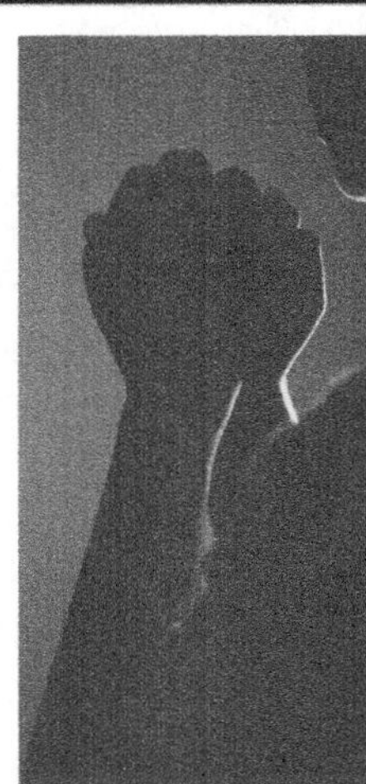

FORGIVE ME, FATHER

Forgive me, Father for I have sinned.
It has been thirty years since my last confession.
I woke with a hunger for terrible things-evil things.
Like the feel of you shattering between my thighs.
And the taste of your blood between your bones

A CHAT WITH

Ashley Michele

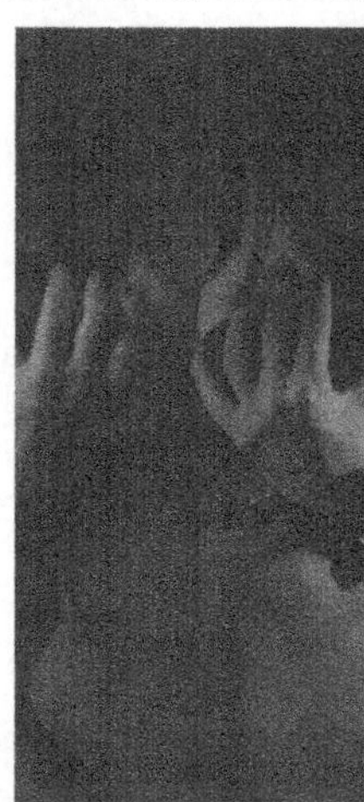

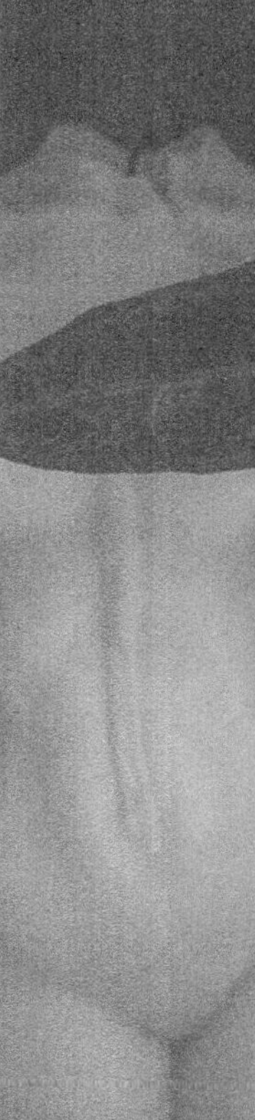

A CHAT WITH ASHLEY MICHELE

ASHLEY MICHELE (SHE/HER/THEY/THEM) IS YOUR neighborhood queer witch. Armed with a BA from Florida State University, Ashley enjoys writing about mixed Latine plus-sized babies (such as herself), talking about kink, and lurking in libraries.

The Hedone editorial team had a chance to sit down and talk with Michele about their writing, their love of horror, and their upcoming novella with Hedone Books, *Forgive Me, Father.*

IT'S NOT UNCOMMON FOR PEOPLE TO BE DISMISSIVE OF erotica and other forms of "chick lit" (a term we hope to make one of empowerment here at Hedone). Why do you think erotica is often overlooked in literary circles or dismissed as "serious" writing?

Maybe it's cliche but I genuinely think it's tied directly to Patriarchy. While erotica isn't solely for women, it is a femme dominated space that is explicit about sex. We still see outdated ideas of men being expected or even encouraged to explore sex while femmes are still called whores and sluts whenever they show enthusiasm for it.

Erotica is an unapologetically sexual space, typically with no moral compunction one way or another, and that threatens the status quo in a way that certain institutionalized ideals can't accept or support because it might endanger the foundation they survive on.

It's funny because no one questions *Lady Chatterley's Lover*, or Shakespeare, or *Lolita*-not in academia. They're seen as completely valid, "serious" works, worthy of analysis and exploration but it's all very explicit and sexual. They're also all written by men. Funny, huh?

HOW IMPORTANT IS IT FOR YOU THAT YOUR WORK explores marginalized identities?

Very! Vital even. At my core, I'm a marginalized human. I'm fat, queer, Latine. I'm mixed, so even in my marginalization, I'm separated from the whole: too white for some people, too 'exotic' for others. I grew up Muslim post 9/11 in the south, I was raised Arab in predominantly white spaces. Nothing about me has ever gone with the flow of society's expectations.

Exploring marginalization, at this point, isn't just about me: it's for Baby Ashley, who didn't have anyone to relate to in the books and media they were consuming. They had to pretend that other girls looked and sounded like her, and thought like her. Had to pretend they had her life experience. Even if I'm not outwardly classifying or honing in on someone's marginalization in my writing, it's there, written in their blood. I think that even having marginalized characters just being the default and the norm, not pointing to it or making a big deal about it is needed.

I take that responsibility very seriously.

HOW DO YOU THINK WE CAN MAKE EROTICA MORE inclusive and accessible for new readers and writers?

Potentially controversial opinion? Quit fucking worrying about the orgasms.

People are so fixated on the end result of sex that they rush to get across the finish line. And then what? It's not a grocery list to get through, and if it is? Consider if it's something you really want or need in your life.

So many people expect sex to look and sound, taste and feel all one way and that's just not the reality. It shouldn't be. For readers and writers both: meet your characters where they're at. If they have back issues, let them do slow exploration in a way that's comfortable. If they can't focus when things are too slow, give them the rough and tumble.

It's so basic, but it's true that people miss the journey when they focus on the end goal. I gave up years ago worrying about why I didn't orgasm the way other people spoke about. I made the conscious decision to remove that as a goal from my sex and my god, what a beautiful experience it became. How fun!

The amount of people who've looked at me with pity when I admit, "I don't orgasm," or freaked the fuck out when it came time to have sex with me and I had to tell them from the jump, "Don't expect this of me." Or who even ask "Uh, where's XYZ character's orgasm?" It's there! It just looks different. If it's not there, why does it need to be? Did they have fun? Did they explore each other's bodies? Did they love everything about it? Then why does it matter?

There's a shame that festers in the expectations of sexual performance. It's something I've worked with a lot with my clients previously in my career with sex work. It keeps people in their feelings in the worst way when they can't meet those expectations and that isn't fair to them. Sex should always be catered and tailored to the individuals experiencing it. It should always be about their pleasure, first and foremost. How you get there doesn't matter. Recognizing that is the first step to making it accessible and pleasurable for everyone.

WHAT ARE SOME OF YOUR BIGGEST SOURCES OF inspiration when it comes to your writing?

Other people's art. There are certain artists I can't consume without my work reflecting it, or without being so immersed into their worlds that I come out with a laundry list of new ideas or I have to put down their work just to write my own. Sometimes it's songs, maybe movies, or books. Sometimes it's just walking past something and feeling a shift in energy that I desperately need to document.

IS THERE A GENRE OR MODE OF STORYTELLING YOU'RE hoping to experiment with in the future?

Southern Gothic! I live in the south. I love the atmosphere, the taste and texture of it. Some of the major elements of Southern Gothic stories are the characters: these deeply flawed humans who are steeped in this ominous fog of tension that kind of rides the line between gritty realism and the fantastical supernatural. It's one of the best modes of social critique I've ever experienced, and that's always something that I find popping up in my own writing.

I made a pact with myself recently to finish a lot of open projects and to then begin moving all the new ones into the south, specifically Northern Florida. I live in a swamp, and people think I'm exaggerating all the time but I'm serious. I want my writing to reflect that beauty. I want people to hear it when they're reading.

***FORGIVE ME, FATHER* IS DARKER AND HAS MORE HORROR elements than your currently published works. What led you to incorporate these elements into this project specifically?**

I think there's a common misconception that horror exists on a spectrum: the more bloody and gore-like the more Horror it is, but I don't quite think that's correct. People who have read *Hush Little Baby* (my first erotic horror) have argued a lot about whether or not it really counts as horror, and I would question why they think it wouldn't be? I wanted it to be very classic in its approach-atmosphere over gore, creeping dread over blood. I think I succeeded in my task!

With *Forgive Me, Father* I really wanted to play with the visceral nature of horror without going so far into the gore that I wouldn't like to read it, or see it in live action. That instead, it might not feel hokey but stay within the lines of sensuality. What better place to put that than in a church?

I don't have the traditional religious trauma other people I have, I don't think. I had a very eclectic religious upbringing. My Grammie is Catholic, my dad is Christian, my mom is Muslim, I'm pagan. But at a young age, in a time where people around me were afraid of Muslims, I was learning to recognize how scary Christians could be-how dismissive of myself and my family in the name of their own God they could become, even people who claimed to love me. It was a sort of one-track hive mind that made you always feel like you were in danger of being eaten up.

I wanted to take that fear and turn it into something tangible, and so that's where the elements come from, I'd say. Imagining this space that's supposed to be loving and caring, but instead is consuming and overpowering but manifested into real danger.

WHAT ARE SOME OF YOUR PROUDEST MOMENTS ALONG your author journey so far?

When I stopped checking reviews, that was a big one. Hitting a million page reads in KU (Kindle Unlimited)-I couldn't believe people had read anything of mine that much. Being here, a part of Hedone. I don't often think of myself as someone other people think about so when they do, I'm never sure if I should be excited or terrified. Every single post someone tags me in. That sounds silly maybe but I look at every single one of them and I think "Oh my God, you actually read it?" When my Grammie left copies of my smut all around her town (including her Church, thanks Grammie).

But I think my proudest moment is when my dad asked me why I hadn't told anyone I was writing, or posted it on my personal Facebook. I'd been writing for a year and I was truthfully trying to keep it from that side of the family. I told him it was smut (in the middle of a Christian Academy school event mind you, with all my family there) just to get him to shut up and he said, 'So?' like it was no big deal. He's always been like that though. Always super proud of what I'm doing even when I think it's dumb or stupid or that he might be mad at it.

Has your involvement with kink education and community transformed how your character development and relationships will play out?

Oh, one hundred percent. My background in kink has transformed how I have platonic relationships let alone how I handle romantic ones. I can't imagine that it doesn't have any effect on how the relationships pan out for my characters. They're often very anxious, depressed, bipolar humans themselves but will still confront someone in ways that other people have deemed "unrealistic" or "out of character" for someone dealing with those mental health issues. I always find that funny, because they're the same issues I deal with, and hold some of the very same truth of how I move in the world.

In kink, and especially from an education perspective there's a directness that just has to be applied. You don't have the luxury of beating around the bush for ages, you have to get in there and be clear about what you're saying, and recognize you're not always going to be right, either but it doesn't make your experience any less valid.

I like to think I do a good job of finding that balance for all my characters.

Thank you so much again for taking the time to speak with us! Can you let everyone know where to find you, and your work, online?

You can find me on Instagram, Threads, and TikTok as AshleyMicheleLx, or over on my website at Ashleymichelelx.com.

ASHLEY MICHELE

"FORGIVE ME, FATHER"

Buried in the mossy swamps of Florida, Forgive Me, Father is a sexually charged novella dripping with power and corruption. Follow as Ava Maria relishes in what it means to devour others, and delights at being devoured in turn.

Ashley Michele is your neighborhood queer little witch. She likes snark, stuffies and dark, fantastical things. She also enjoys writing about mixed Latine plus-sized babies (such as herself) getting to live out their best lives with queer and kinky loving.

She has a BA from Florida State University that she still hasn't opened. When she's not doing library things or sending hour-long voice notes to someone she loves, she can usually be found in her hammock between the trees of her swamp or listening to an audiobook while she paints and catches some sun.

For more, check out her website at Ashleymichelelx.com or on social media under the handle @ashleymichelelx.

Sapphire Lazuli

O, BUT TO BE

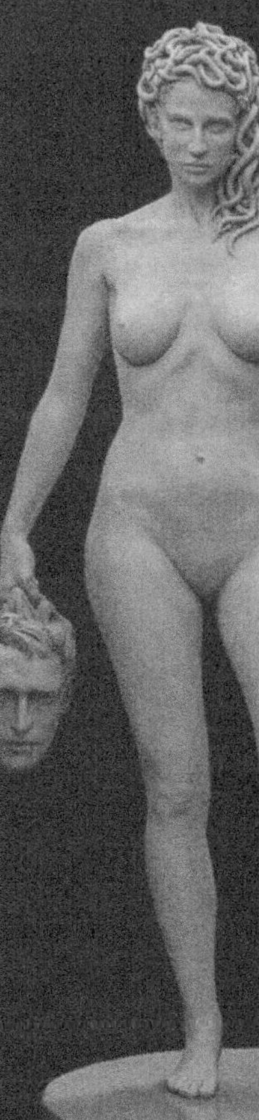

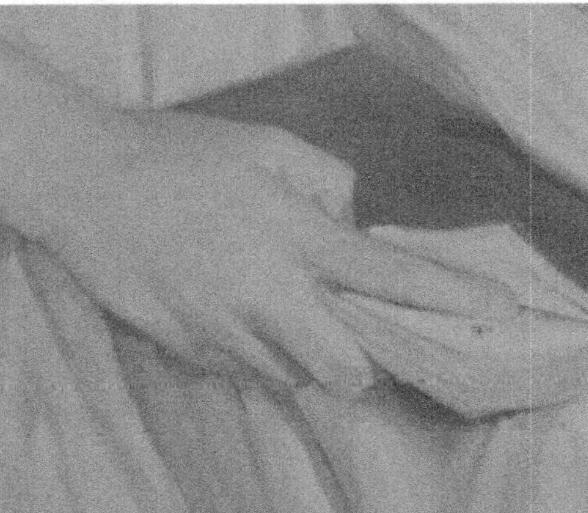

O, BUT TO BE

There is nudity in absence.
Struck bare is she taken alone,
Clothed only now in woven want.

Rear made sky is but a bright void in the moonlight,
And I, a daft shadow consumed by dust.
Bricks lathed as walls,
Embrace the naked me,
And eyes as broken bow strings lay flaccid,
Against Gaze, unbalanced arrow.
In that it were not here to which attempts are made,
I'll hold the thought that I might propel the Weapon.

What man are you? *To nothing air I do beseech.*
Rippled crystal as runny and as wet as rain is, like the bricks, a wall.
My salty spout for residue.

Dust of dusk to mine ample face,
Bathed thus in which I am to grant advent.

To thee, nie saying horse, dark stallion as grim as Night,
Should I look from whence I stand and whisper,
O' she doth court the scythe

And with these words stained 'pon my lips wouldst thou think to,
In the absence of what you have reaped,
Kiss them?
If only that in touch I might,
Like stricken soldiers past,
Lay down my broken and dead self within where I had yearned.

SAPPHIRE LAZULI

"SQUIRM, YOU PRECIOUS THING."

Imagine desire as a hundred frayed silk threads. In such is created tableaus: a witch who squeals to know the true authority of gods; a bastard boy, made wet as mud and worms and blood; in some Scottish *play a Lady howls at the sight of herself; and alone, made a widow by the whims of men, a woman chases a name for the sun. Sapphire* Lazuli's collection, Squirm, You Precious Thing, *serves as a beautiful and experimental introduction to* Lazuli's *lyrical style, interweaving poetry and prose.*

Sapphire Lazuli (she/they), Author of *Our Witchless Flesh* (Coming 2025 via Off Limits Press) and writer/director of *Haunted Houses and Houses That Haunt* and *Those Were The Days*, is an artist whose brush is dipped in weird horror and perverted desires. Their prose is often described as beautifully poetic and adjacent to the reader; Sapphire does not write stories that will hold your hand. Be it cosmic entities appearing as places, gross and erotic explorations of the boundaries of form, deep dives into the darkest ridges of the mind and desire, or even video essays divulging the many mechanisms that construct fear, her horror is bound to allure you.

THE NEST OF...

Damien Casey

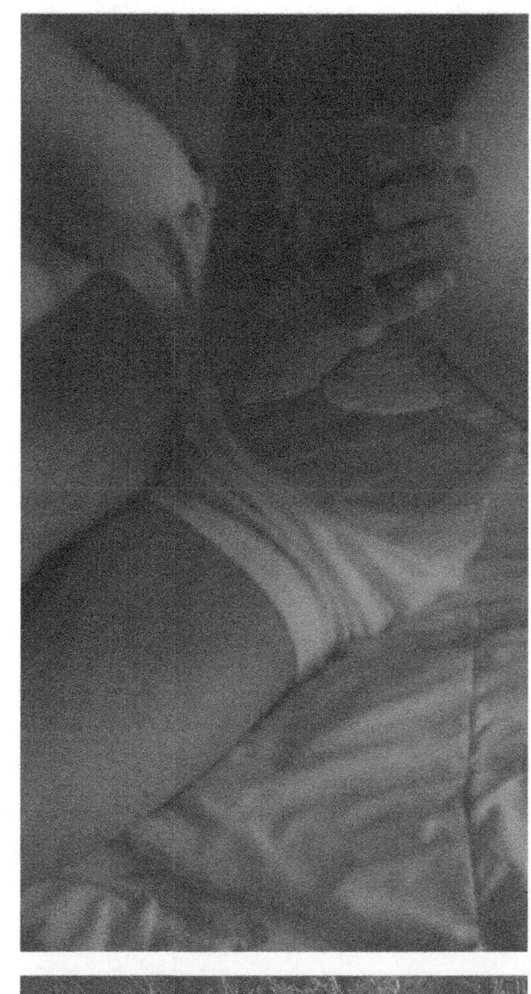

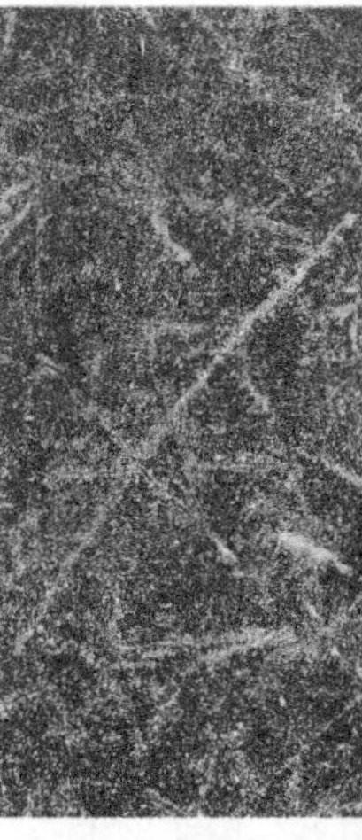

THE NEST OF...

HE FOUND HER THROUGH A SEARCH, "AMATEUR HOMEMADE threesome," on a porn site. He was looking for something real, something genuine. He was tired of the same old pornstars with the same fake tits, fake orgasms, fake asses, and fake emotions. The same muscle dudes with 1950's dad haircuts plowing away at them for forty-five minutes. At some point, it turned into an unending loop of watching Barbie and Ken fuck.

The thumbnail shook Curt right to his core: a girl in doggystyle on a sofa with a guy penetrating her from behind while another one was getting a blowjob, his head back and eyes closed as casually as if he was getting a pedicure. He could instantly feel his dick growing when he looked at the title "Wife Takes TWO!!! Cocks For The First Time!!!" He knew if he masturbated right now, he'd be late to work. He only had five minutes, but Curt suspected he couldn't even last two.

He clicked the link.

She appeared to be in her late thirties and looked nothing like the women his friends watched. She was the kind of woman you would bump into at a grocery store. She hadn't dedicated her life to the male gaze and it made him feel crazier. She was the kind of woman you'd see every day and lust after. Someone with a real life. Someone with actual emotion.

When it started, the woman–Alicia–took up the whole screen as she propped up a home video camera before backing up to the sofa.

The two men then appeared on screen. They were the kind of guys who had other things to do than get paid to be naked.

The scene was awkward at first. The woman stuck to her husband for the most part, while the other man sat there masturbating and watching the couple have sex. They switched positions and her husband took her from behind while his friend slid into position next to her. The woman was visibly nervous but she reached out and took the other man in her hand and slowly stroked him. Tension flowed from the screen. He felt as though he were being filled up with it like a hungry plant soaking up sunlight. The woman looked at the camera for a split second and then took the other man in her mouth.

Curt exploded. He'd waited the whole video for that moment. When she finally did it, the tone of the video completely changed. One minute it was awkward, the next it was a frenzy of sexual freedom. He sat there and watched the rest of the video.

Curt was in love.

He had to know more about this woman.

He browsed around their profile and found other videos. Some scenes involved more than one man. These weren't models or professionals, these were average people making porn for fun. He started wondering about their lives. Did their co-workers, friends, and families know about these videos? Would they even mention it to the couple on camera if they did?

"Hey bro, I was wanking before work, and I stumbled across you and your wife going at it."

No, he didn't think they would.

He browsed a bit longer and found a video called "Alicia's FIRST Lesbian SexXx!!!"

He hovered the mouse over the link when he caught a glimpse of the time. It hit him like a brick. He was a half hour late and hadn't even gotten dressed yet. He bookmarked the video and ran to get ready.

CURT COULDN'T STOP THINKING ABOUT HER ALL DAY.

Alicia.

Alicia. Alicia. Alicia.

AliciaAliciaAliciaAlicia

What does she do?

Where does she live?

Was he crossing paths with people like her all day?

How would he know if he was?

When a co-worker walked behind him, he couldn't help but wonder if she's like Alicia.

What if she's at home getting fucked by her husband and another guy?

He found himself thinking of the men he bumped into that way too; seeing every man as someone's husband, or someone's husband's friend, in a video on the internet.

He couldn't erase her name from his head. Every person he called for work, every person he tried to sell a fake plastic Amish-made fireplace to, he thought, *Alicia? Could this be her?*

He was suddenly glad his job involved him sitting at a desk and calling people for eight hours. Although his dick hurt from being hard all day, it was a relief to at least be able to hide it.

AS SOON AS HE GOT HOME, HE WENT RIGHT TO THE bookmarked video.

The drive home from work was rough. He felt like he was driving drunk; his mind was so distracted.

It opened with Alicia. Her brown hair was tied back into a sloppy ponytail and she wore a white T-shirt and jeans. She was softly kissing another woman with brown hair.

He sat there in shock.

It was perfection.

The awkwardness was thick in this video as well. As they lightly made out and caressed each other's breasts, the tension was too strong for Curt and he skipped forward three minutes. The scene changed to both women shirtless, kissing and lightly groping each other. Alicia reached around the other woman's back and undid her bra. As soon as her breasts were free, Curt was done.

He felt slightly empty this time, the euphoria he felt at the first video replaced with longing and need. He had to know who these people were and where he could find them.

He had to.

WHEN HE SLEPT, HE DREAMT OF A LOW-LIT ROOM. THE SMELL of cheap candles. Alicia standing in front of him. A man with a camera off to the side.

"Ok baby, this is weird for me too, but the viewers want some fan videos so we're going to make one for them."

Slowly, Alicia undid his pants and pulled his dick out. She took him in her mouth and within minutes he came. He felt himself nearly scream out, instead settling for a long groan as his fantasies were fulfilled. She didn't pause or slow down, and instead just swallowed his cum and kept at it.

He came over and over again.

When Alicia finally came up for some air after the fifth–or maybe it was the sixth–time, he saw the inside of her mouth was covered in blood. He looked down at his cock, the length of it looking as though he had tattooed it entirely red. Her mouth encapsulated him again and he couldn't move. Paralyzed by fear and worry about what had happened to his cock, he watched frozen as she sucked on him for a few minutes before detaching from his groin.

"Why are you limp, baby? Don't worry about the blood. It's just a dream, you're just fantasizing about this. I would NEVER suck you off in real life. But for now, I guess it's fine."

She took him in her mouth again and a jolt of lightning shot through him, her teeth grinding his flesh and muscle into nothing.

Eyes open. Fear. Pain.

He quickly threw the covers off and looked at his genitals. No blood.

HE SAT THERE FOR HOURS WATCHING VIDEOS, TRYING TO FIND some clue about where they lived, what town they were from.

"Alicia Gives Hubby Head on FREEWAY!!!"

This would be the one. Surely he'd be able to spot a sign on the side of the road or even catch a glimpse of a license plate.

It didn't take long for him to find what he was looking for.

GLENN'S FURNITURE EMPORIUM. BEND, WEST VIRGINIA.

The sign was barely a smudge in the background, but it was there.

Curt had a city.

From what he remembered, the town of Bend was a pretty small

operation. No real attractions. A few gas stations, a grocery store, and, of course, the furniture emporium. It was also only five hours from home and he had the day off tomorrow.

He studied the video to see if he could tell what kind of car they were driving. The inside made it obvious it was a four door. At one point, he could see in the rear-view mirror that it was red. At another, he caught the logo on the steering wheel. He had the color, make, and model. Probably about two hundred of those in a small town.

Great.

This would be easy as pie.

He kept watching videos to get a hint of where their home was in Bend. Curt couldn't help but wonder if the couch in so many of their videos was from Glenn's Furniture Emporium. He giggled at the prospect. He figured that the worst case scenario is that he'd drive five hours to be in the same store where Alicia had bought her couch and jack off in the bathroom, or maybe even on the floor model if nobody was watching. It wouldn't be the same as meeting her, but it would be a thrill nonetheless.

As he browsed the videos, he got a better picture of her home. In one video–"Alicia Gives OFFICE HEAD!!!"–he could see a large building and a forklift close to their home from one of the massive windows. It was all he needed. He typed "Industrial plants, Bend, West Virginia" into the search bar and found the same building. It was a recycling center. He wrote down the address; that's where he'd start.

Despite the plan, Curt couldn't wait any longer.

So he didn't.

HIS BODY WAS SHAKING AS HE DROVE. MORE THAN ONCE HE felt himself drifting onto the shoulder of the road as his mind wandered. He got to the recycling center a little before midnight, unaware of the time that had passed.

He drove around the block a couple of times but couldn't find anything. He was almost giving up when, on the fourth pass, he found the red four-door sitting in a driveway outside a small single-wide mobile home. He'd driven by the house a few times already, but the car hadn't been there and the lights hadn't been on before.

Someone must have just arrived.

Maybe Alicia's in there.

The thought made him hard and before he could stop himself, he'd masturbated in the driver's seat, his eyes glued on Alicia's house the whole time.

Needing more, he went and knocked.

"Hello?" a voice said from behind the door.

"Hey, I know this seems weird... Well, maybe it's just weird to me. I'm sure this happens to you all the time. But, uh, I was wondering if Alicia was home?"

"No, I'm sorry she's not here, we ugh, spli- wait, who are you again?"

"My name's Curt, I'm sort of a.... well.... fan"

"A fan?"

"Yeah, I've, well, the thing is...I'll be straight up. I've seen your videos on a porn site an-"

"Get the fuck out of here."

"Hey, sorry I didn-" Curt backed away from the door as if it were the voice yelling.

"You get the fuck out of here before I kick the shit out of you, drag you inside, and call the cops to tell them you tried to rob me, you fucking pervert."

He uploads videos fucking his girl for the public to see and then gets mad when the public shows up? What a dick.

Curt made his way back to his car and shoved the keys in the ignition. He didn't close the door until after he took off. The door almost slamming shut from the momentum of takeoff irritated him with himself. He took off down the street, muttering angrily to himself under his breath about how he couldn't focus. His stomach gurgled so he cut through traffic to a fast food place on the other side of the road. Car horns rang out and he felt himself getting more and more annoyed.

First no Alicia, then I get treated like a fucking freak.

Curt rolled his window down as he pulled up to the speaker. He hated ordering through a drive-thru speaker but he had no time. It crackled and popped before an employee's voice rang out in a listless monotone.

"Billy's Burger Bar. What can I get you?"

As he placed his order–he hated eating in his car but cheese-

burgers were easy to carry–a thought formed in the back of his mind causing a smile to play across his face. Excitedly, he paid for his food and took off back up the street, suddenly in a hurry to get back to Alicia's house.

A KNOCK.

Is this fucking creep back?

Andy had finally started to calm down after the man left, but now here it was again. That familiar feeling of anxiety at the back of his throat.

Can't a man just sit around and get drunk all evening?

He gets up and goes to the door, dreading whoever's behind it. There was a takeout bag and drink sitting in front of his door with a note that said "Sorry."

Little fucker's trying to apologize, huh?

Andy neither saw nor felt the blow to the back of his head when he bent down for his gift.

"YOU'VE PUT ON SOME WEIGHT. I'M A LITTLE SHOCKED. YOU guys had a video a day for a couple of months back there. That should have worked the fat off you, right Andy?" Curt held up a wallet to punctuate his statement. He grinned as he saw the realization cross Andy's face.

"What is this?"

"Duct tape," he said, holding up the silver roll.

"I can see that. I mean, what's the situation here?"

"Oh, right. Surely you know what a hostage is."

"A hostage? For what? I've got no fucking cash. I was going to eat the poisoned food you left-"

A solid punch.

"Now look Andrew, I don't want any money. Nah. This is my day off and I just want to have some fun. You acted like such a dick earlier. You could have just told me Alicia didn't live here and sent me on my way."

"Right. Great idea. Tell a complete stranger where my ex-wife lives. Gotcha. 'Hey Alicia I know we had a nasty divorce, but some guy uploaded our private videos to a porn site and now some sick fuck is here looking for you. I hope you don't mind, but I gave him your address!' Great fucking idea."

Curt stomped down hard on Andy's foot, bones crunching from the force. Andy's head rolled back, his teeth grinding together as his writs strained against the duct tape that kept him trapped in the wooden chair. He dug his nails into the seat, splinters entering the soft flesh beneath them.

"Buddy! I got you trapped and you think you're the one who can talk shit?"

Andy decided he was done talking and instead began wondering how long it would take someone to find him. On the one hand, if he didn't show up for work tomorrow evening, they'd send someone to check on him.. On the other hand, he sincerely hoped it wouldn't take that long for help to arrive.

"Look man, I don't work until noon tomorrow, so we've got the whole day to sort this shit out." Curt frantically scratched at his scalp, waiting for Andy to reply.

He didn't.

"Where does Alicia live? If you tell me, I'm just going to drive over there and introduce myself. That's it! I'll come back, clean you up, and head home. Does that sound like a deal?"

Andy just stared blankly out the window behind Curt.

"Look man, hitting you with the butt of that gun felt great and, *honestly*, it's taking everything in my power not to do it again. If you don't tell me, I'm just going to kill you, and I'll find out where she lives another way. So, you know, you scratch my back and I don't shoot you in yours."

"I don't know where she is."

"Bullshit."

"You looked through my house. You found my gun. Did you see anything with her name on it? She left two years ago after my phone was stolen. Alicia was convinced that I'd sold our videos to someone and lied to her about it. So forgive me for being a little agitated when you show up talking about videos that ruined my marriage."

"You fucking liar," Curt said, pointing the gun at Andy.

"If I knew where she was, I'd be there.," Andy said, raising his head in defiance. "She went to stay with her sister somewhere in Tennessee. I don't even know what town she's in."

Andy's phone began buzzing on the coffee table, the name *Alicia* taking up the whole screen.

"I knew you were a fucking liar. Answer it and tell her to come home," Curt said as he slammed the butt of the gun down on Andy's genitals, crushing them against the hard seat of the chair.

Andy screamed in pain, his muscles clenching and bulging against his restraints.

"Hey, you're on speakerphone," he managed between gasps "There's a guy here who says if you don't come home, he'll kill me."

"Well," replied Alicia, "did you tell him that isn't possible?"

"I don't think he cares."

"Oh, even better. Hey, weird rapey killer guy," she said, suddenly addressing Curt, "I'll be there in a few seconds."

The line went dead.

Curt looked at Andy with confusion as the line went dead.

"A few seconds? Is she next fucking do-"

Pain shot through his stomach before he could finish the sentence. He looked down and there was a blade sticking out the front of his shirt covered in blood. He gasped and fell over onto the couch (the one he suspected was from Bob's Furniture Emporium).

He watched as Andy casually undid his duct tape and stood up, took off his shoe and poured out a mess of blood and crushed bone onto Curt's lap.

"Damn, look at this mess you did to my foot! I knew you were going to be a good one when you tried to poison me."

"That food wasn't poison-" Curt couldn't force the words out of his mouth. This time when he looked down the knife was gone, and Alicia had shoved three fingers crudely into the wound.

"It really sucks how this went, Curt," Alicia said. "Usually, they give up and fuck off after Andy tells them I've left. And then sometimes I'll show up and fuck them for being at least a little respectable."

"She's always liked playing with her food," Andy chuckled.

"But this?" she asked, widening her fingers and stretching the wound. "This is the part you don't see on camera. Once the video ends, you all end up the same way."

"What are you?"

"Succubus. Incubus. Demon. Devil. The name doesn't matter. It never has. What matters is that you all fall in love with us, because that's what looking at us does to you. You all want more. You all *need* more. And so you find the clues, make your way here, and never realize that this was *our* plan all along."

Alicia began working her fingers deeper inside Curt's chest. She pushed the red slicked fingers in and pulled them out, pushed them in deeper, pulled them out, and then forced her entire fist in the open gash. Curt screamed, but couldn't peel his eyes away from her. She continued to work him open, reaching her hand deeper inside, as Andy grabbed her hips with his hands and pressed himself against her, before feeling her chest over her clothes.

Curt could feel her hand tighten around something inside of his chest, but he didn't care. He was too busy watching Alicia rock her hips back against another man, moaning to herself with unmet need.

With a cry of release, she pulled her arm from his chest, his heart clenched firmly in her hand. She moaned as she brought his heart up to her lips and took a bite. Curt smiled, his eyes unfocusing and his breathing coming to a stop.

He was finally hers.

He was finally inside the woman he loved.

DAMIEN CASEY

"YEAR OF THE FOX"

Isabelle White knows two things for sure: it's her job to hunt the demons that no one else can and that she's going to be damned if she doesn't have a good time–and a few orgasms–doing it. Over the course of a year, Isabelle will discover her power, herself, and what it means to be human.

Damien Casey writes mostly horror comedy inspired by the b-movies of the 80's. He was born when two VHS tapes melted together in the sun.

FEED THE TREE

Wendy Dalrymple

FEED THE TREE

CHAPTER ONE

1889

Small pleasures are precious and few for those who make their living off the land. The palmetto scrub forest that surrounds our farm is thick and vast, with only the music of the insects and birds to keep me company. In the summer the humidity bears down like a wet, wool blanket, making a body long for the relief of an autumn breeze. Some days it seems like there isn't much to look forward to other than more sweat, blood and pain. Some days I wonder if there's anything worth living for at all.

I am only twenty but this life makes me feel far older than my years. Then, again, Mama always did say I am an old soul. I try hard to be a good person, but deep down, something bad beats at my chest like dark feathered wings against a rusted cage. Sinister thoughts often invade my mind, and more than once I've given in to them. I find that I have to keep myself busy and focused at all times. If I am distracted, if

I work hard and give to everyone but myself, it's easier to keep those bad thoughts and inclinations at bay.

Tending to the animals and the garden, cleaning the house and caring for Daddy leaves me drained of energy and ambition. The hours are long and hot on our farmstead at the edge of the swamp, and the hardships often outweigh the easy times. Mosquitos the size of pennies bite at any tender flesh I leave exposed, little demons determined to bleed their victims dry. Since they don't have proper shade and water, our crops wither and die easily. Wild animals with sharp teeth wander freely in the forest and waterways, so I must not let our livestock roam. The settlers who pushed their way into this stolen land knew that living here wouldn't be easy or pleasant. It was never a life I would have planned for myself. Unlike the settlers, I wasn't given a choice.

After Mama died five years back, Daddy completely lost all interest in living at all. He took to the bottle like others in mourning have done before him, neglecting everything including me. I didn't blame him at first. I was in mourning too, although I had no one to comfort me. My wants and needs didn't matter anymore as I worked to keep us both alive. Instead of planning for my future, I watched the days fall off the calendar one by one, dropping like unanswered wishes from plucked flower petals.

Despite all of my troubles, I allow myself one small pleasure. Henry. The only person I've ever truly loved. My time with him is special and secret, all tangled limbs and sweaty bed sheets, tongues in places that would make any parishioner blush. Henry sneaks through my window on Saturday nights after I've finished all my chores and tucked Daddy into bed. All week long I yearn for the weight of him, anxious to inhale the sun-dried scent of his clothes and taste the briny salt of his skin. I can't tell anyone about our time together of course, for obvious reasons.

Henry has been dead for nearly a year.

I met Henry down at the docks, where everyone in town gathers to sell their wares, trade and share the latest gossip. Every now and then, I'm able to earn a few extra coins selling wild honey and beautyberry jam, which go for a higher price than our usual eggs, butter and squash. Once a month I go to town on my own to sell my produce and trade for flour, sugar, coffee and Daddy's medicine. Whatever money was leftover I used to buy fish that the boats had brought in that day. The scallops and shrimp were a nice change from our usual diet of chicken, greens, corn cakes, grits and salted pork. I enjoyed treating myself to delicacies from the sea, but I looked forward to seeing Henry more.

Everyone in town knew about my circumstances, but few showed me kindness. The men there were hardened by life in a different way than I was and that hardness often manifested as cruelty. Not Henry though. Henry was a gentleman and always had a smile for me. Sometimes he would even give me a little extra fish in my bucket for smoking and drying. One day a spoke on my wagon wheel broke when I was at the docks and he helped me repair it, but by then, I was already smitten. Henry came out to the cabin to see me that very night. He brought me so much joy and showed me there was more to the world than loneliness, sadness and pain.

My time with Henry was blissful, but short-lived. That summer, a tropical storm took out half the fleet of shrimp boats, his vessel, *The Lucky Lady*, among them. Search parties went out to look for survivors after the unexpected storm, but there was little hope for him or the other men who worked the docks. Henry's body was likely somewhere among the wreckage, lost to the depths of the Gulf of Mexico, but his spirit returned to me just the same.

Our first night together after he died is etched into my memory. Our possible future together was all that I had to look forward to, and in a flash, it was gone. Weeks of silent suffering and loss had built up inside of me, my pain crystalized and aching to burst free. I was at my breaking point. Without Henry in it, the world was bleaker than ever. I was nearly ready to end my own life and join him and Mama in the hereafter when I heard a tapping on my window pane.

I wasn't sure what I was seeing at first, of course. No one believes their dead lover will return to them, certainly not anyone of sound mind. Yet, there he was, waiting outside my window just like always. Henry passed through the glass like a vapor as I laid still in my bed, too terrified to move. His touch was cold at first, wet against my fevered brow. His hand traced down my collarbone, my skin taught and awakened under his unearthly touch. I should have been afraid, but I wasn't. It was my Henry, after all. He would never hurt me.

But then, something changed. In spirit form, he approached me more aggressively than ever before. I gasped as the ties at the bodice of my nightgown gave way, undone as though by invisible hands. My breasts were exposed in the soft moonlight as his watery form hovered over me. I was terrified in that moment and also — it shames me to admit — enticed.

I welcomed his cold, wet hands as they worked around my nipples. My body responded as his spirit bore a strange weight down upon me. He still smelled like sunshine and the sea as his ghostly hand snaked between my thighs. Even though his touch was cold, my body warmed to him just the same.

I always knew it would be a risk to fall in love with someone who worked at the docks; the very nature of being a fisherman is dangerous at its core. But I didn't know how strong our love would become, how even death couldn't keep us apart. That is why I was so desperate to bring his bodily form back.

That's why I needed to venture out into the swamp and find Her.

CHAPTER TWO

My hometown of Carabelle was a small fishing community on the Gulf Coast of Florida's panhandle, newly incorporated like many other places in this wild region. Ever since I was a girl, making friends my own age proved to be almost impossible. Even if I had time to socialize, there were few honest, good people in town, and even fewer young women. Perhaps loneliness is what drove me to attend service at Chapel by the Sea. Despite being raised by a devout mother, I lost my faith long ago and had no interest in being saved or learning about heaven and hell. Other than the monthly market at the docks, church was the one place where I could at least see flesh and blood people, catch up on gossip and get help when I needed it. It was also the only place I could see Sissy.

Sissy was the daughter of Preacher Jacobs and his wife, Milicent. She was a year younger than me and my only friend in town. Though we were as different as peach and pecan pie, Sissy and I understood each other. She was every bit the portrait of a preacher's daughter, flagrant against the word of God and a holy terror in her own right. I was lucky to have found her. We were bound by the fact that there was something inherently bad in us both. Though we tried to be good, she and I leaned toward dark things. Rotten things.

It was Sissy who told me about Agatha in the first place.

On the last Sunday in August I decided to ask her about the swamp witch. Church seemed just a fitting place as any to inquire about the local magical creature who resided on the outskirts of town. That morning the parishioners lingered in the lobby of the chapel later than usual, soaking up the last of the shade before their long treks home. I needed to get back to Daddy, but my curiosity and loneliness kept me lingering too. I was bursting at the seams all morning in anticipation of meeting up with my friend to ask that which should not be asked. I held my breath and tapped on her shoulder.

"Sissy. I have a question."

"What's that?" Sissy tucked a stray lock of ebony hair behind one ear as she turned to face me. Her translucent complexion and dark, cat-like eyes were a stark contrast to my ruddy, sunburned cheeks and wheat-colored hair. She was wearing a new blue and white gingham dress that likely came from her aunt's shop in Savannah. Next to her I looked rather homely, though she never made me feel that way.

"I need you to tell me how to find... Her."

"Who?" Sissy asked.

"You know. The woman in the swamp."

"Oh, you mean Agatha."

I nodded, and Sissy leaned in closer. Her thick, dark lashes fluttered as she glanced about the room. She pursed her lips in a conspiratorial smile and leaned in to whisper in my ear. My heart blipped as she wrapped a slender hand around my arm, the scent of rosewater enveloping my senses.

"She lives way out past the big bend, inside the hollow of a lightning-struck oak tree."

"What does she look like?" I asked.

"She has hooves for feet, just like a javelina, and her hair drapes long and ashen gray like moss. And her eyes! They glow like fire."

"Stop kidding," I scoffed. "Seriously, what does she look like?"

"I am being serious!" Sissy frowned. "I wouldn't lie to you."

"I know you wouldn't," I whispered, her hair brushing against my lips. "Well, have you ever known anyone who has gone to see her then?"

"No." Sissy gazed into my eyes, her dark pupils sparkling. "But I heard that if you bring her an offering, she'll grant you a wish."

"Like what?"

Sissy shrugged. "Homemade bread. Honey. Flowers. I don't know, something nice."

"I could do that," I said.

"Are you still having your spells?" Sissy asked, her usually smooth forehead lined in what I could tell was worry. "Or is it for your father?"

"No," I shook my head. "Daddy is fine. I just need something."

"I know you've been having a hard time since Henry—"

"Ladies." Preacher Jacobs appeared behind his daughter, his face painted with an expression of unmasked disappointment.

"Afternoon, Preacher," I said.

"Don't recall seeing you lately at the women's auxiliary," he said, issuing me the same disappointed glance.

"She has to care for her father, remember?" Sissy said, her coy demeanor now replaced by that of the obedient daughter.

"That's right." He pulled a handkerchief from his breast pocket and dabbed at his glistening brow. "We'll pray for you both. If you'll excuse me, I need to speak to one of the parishioners."

"Thank you, Preacher." I held my breath and waited until I was certain he was out of earshot before turning to Sissy again. "How do you know so much about her anyway?"

Sissy linked arms with me and led me out of the church into the late morning sunlight.

"When I was little, I heard stories about the woman who lived at the edge of the swamp. Her name was Agatha, though all the kids at the schoolhouse used to call her Hagatha. Old grannies and aunties would venture into the swamp and pay her a visit to ask for favors if someone was sick or if their cow's milk ran dry. Men weren't allowed to set foot in her swamp without permission though."

"What would happen if they did?"

"Nothing good," Sissy said. "Word has it that old Cebe Tate did her wrong some years back. She turned into a panther to lure him into the swamp and drove him mad."

I nodded, listening intently. In the past, I would have been far too sensible to believe such stories, but nightly visits from my deceased beloved had opened up my eyes to the world. I needed help and was willing to believe just about anything if it meant I could have Henry back.

"I heard about Cebe Tate," I said. "I thought he was just an old drunk."

"He certainly was, but that doesn't mean it didn't happen. The

ladies quilting circle in town told me all about how Agatha tortured that man for seven days straight before turning him loose. He crawled out of the swamp naked and bloody, spouting nonsense."

"Why did she let him go?" I asked.

Sissy shrugged. "No one knows, least of all old Cebe Tate. I think she did it as a warning."

"A warning?" I asked. "For what?"

"To warn everyone in Carrabelle. I think Agatha let old Cebe Tate live so she could foster fear in the hearts of men."

"So you think she's still out there?" I asked. "Agatha?"

Sissy glanced toward the dirt road in the direction away from town, toward Tate's Hell. Her pink lips spread into a smile and she fluttered those thick lashes at me. "There's only one way to find out."

WENDY DALRYMPLE

"FEED THE TREE"

How far would you go for love?

Alone in the wilds of the Florida Panhandle, a young woman is tormented by the ghost of her secret lover as she cares for her dying father. Desperate to save herself from heartache and the financial ruin promised to an unmarried woman in 1880s America, she turns to a swamp witch who agrees to bring her dead lover back to life with one condition... she must lure unexpecting men into the swamp to fulfill her dark needs.

Wendy Dalrymple loves to explore the beauty in horrific things. When she's not writing femme-focused horror, you can find her hiking with her family, painting (bad) wall art, and trying to grow as many pineapples as possible.

Follow her on Instagram and TikTok under the handle @wendydalrymplewrites.

Sylvester Barzey

A CHAT WITH

A CHAT WITH SYLVESTER BARZEY

SYLVESTER BARZEY (HE/HIM) IS A BEST-SELLING HORROR AND fantasy author who's best known for his *Planet Dead* series. A military veteran with an addiction to all things horror, Sylvester's goal is to centre BIPOC characters within speculative fiction and promote marginalized voices in the community.

The Hedone editorial team had a chance to sit down and talk with Barzey about his fascination with zombies, his love of horror, and his upcoming anthology with Hedone Books, *Undead Lovers*.

THANK YOU SO MUCH FOR TAKING THE TIME TO TALK TO US at Hedone Books! You have an impressive bibliography and we'd be remiss if we didn't ask you about your *Planet Dead* universe! How did that come about and what inspired you to create it?

Hey, thanks for having me. Wow, I never really thought about my bibliography. I look at people like Christopher Artinian and Camille Picott who, when I started, were just knocking out books and I'd think… I'm moving too slow, but I guess I have made a little dent with mine. *Planet Dead* was kind of like an inevitable step for me. I've always enjoyed writing and I'm a big slasher and zombie movie fan. So, I knew if I was ever gonna write a book it was gonna be a horror book and most likely it was gonna have zombies in it.

I started *Planet Dead* in 2010, and while many might find this hard to believe, I never read the *Walking Dead* at that time... so put your lawyers away Robert Kirkman. I wanted to start and finish a project, cause at the time I had a real problem with starting things and not seeing them through. So I decided I was gonna write a book and to ease my mind I pretended each chapter was a short story. The *Planet Dead* that's out now is really far from the one I first started and that might be for the best; I was telling three stories at once and it got big and messy. I think my biggest inspiration for *Planet Dead* was really the thought of making a badass final girl like Sidney (*Scream*), Sarah (*Terminator 2*) and Jeryline (*Demon Knight*) , someone that you know is gonna raise hell before the story is done. That was my inspiration and main focus, building a perfect final girl.

WHAT DO YOU FEEL IS THE MAIN SOURCE OF INSPIRATION for your fiction? Does it vary project to project, or is it more of a constant source for everything?

I would say it varies from project to project. Sometimes I see something in a movie or read something in a book and I wonder "Can I pull this off" and then I go write. The wife and I are really big on true crime, so sometimes I'll hear a case and I build a whole different story around it. I think a lot of my projects have some real world events tied into them. Like in *Planet Dead Book One*, we run into three cannibalistic clowns and they're modeled off of three real life serial killers. I think the very last way I come up with things is that sometimes I'm just making movies in my head. I'll picture how something starts and how it ends, and then if I think it's a really good idea, I'll sit down and fill in the rest.

. . .

You post a lot on social media about the importance of diversity in media. What are some of your favourite works in horror that you think get inclusivity and representation right?

Hmm, that's hard, sometimes I don't feel all that smart on some subject matters, so I don't know if I could say "this book gets it right" but I can tell you some of the books I've read that I felt seen in:

- *Chain-Gang All-Stars* by Nana Kwame Adjei-Brenyah
- *Blood Like Magic* by Liselle Sambury
- *I Feed Her To The Beast And The Beast Is Me* by Jamison Shea
- *Razorblade Tears* by S. A. Cosby
- *The Getaway* by Lamar Giles
- *The Weight Of Blood* by Tiffany D. Jackson

I think each of those books told a unique story that wouldn't have been the same if it didn't come from a marginalized author. They crafted a cast that felt to me like the real world. So I don't know if they got it right but I love em'.

We at Hedone Books are extremely excited to be working with you on the upcoming horror-erotica and dark romance anthology, *Undead Lovers*, that's planned for 2025. What drew you to the idea?

I think the stars really aligned with this project 'cause at the time, I was starting to work on an erotica series with my wife and I was getting interested in dark romance due to all the time I spend on TikTok. So when I saw this opportunity I thought "this is gonna be a lot of fun." I've been given the keys to what I think can be a very beautiful and messed up anthology.

If someone wanted to get a better idea of the type

of work you're looking for, which books or authors would you encourage they check out?

I want beautiful stories with really fucked up concepts or just something that really gives a gut punch to the reader.

- *Tender Is The Flesh* by Agustina Bazterrica
- *Deadgirl* (2008)
- *Return Of The Living Dead 3* (1993)
- *Mexican Gothic* by Silvia Moreno-Garcia
- *Brother* by Ania Ahlborn
- *Secrets Of A Side Bitch* by Jessica N. Watkins

I want the passion and the love to be imprinted on the page but I also want readers to stop and be like "What the hell am I reading? ... And is there more?"

WHEN IT COMES TO THIS SUBMISSION CALL, WHAT ARE some of the things that you're hoping to see in the stories for consideration? What's on your manuscript wish list, so to speak?

I like that! I have a manuscript wish list everyone! I want unique stories, something that really makes me sit and be like "I never thought of that." I want stories that aren't afraid to go to dark places, be it violence or bloody body parts. But if you're gonna do violent things to someone, lets try doing it the guy. We don't see men get fucked up enough in dark romance, if you ask me. And I want spice, like ghost pepper hot.

IS THERE ANY FINAL ADVICE YOU'D LIKE TO GIVE prospective authors ahead of sending work to this submission call?

Writing should always be fun, if you're not having fun then don't stress yourself out. We're not going anywhere and you can try out for another project. Maybe read some messed up romance stories, watch *Returning Of The Living Dead 3*, and see if you have something running around in your head that fits the bill.

THANK YOU SO MUCH AGAIN FOR TAKING THE TIME TO speak with us! Can you let everyone know where to find you, and your work, online?

Sure, you can find me at WWW.SylvesterBarzey.Com and on all social media outlets as @SylvesterBarzey.

SYLVESTER BARZEY

"UNDEAD LOVERS"

Sylvester Barzey is a best-selling horror and fantasy author who grew up in Bronx, NY, and was later transplanted to Bethlehem, GA. A military veteran with an addiction to all things horror, Sylvester's goal is to shine a spotlight on BIPOC characters within the horror/fantasy genre.

You can find Sylvester at: www.sylvesterbarzey.com

Submission Call

UNDEAD LOVERS

edited by

Sylvester Barzey

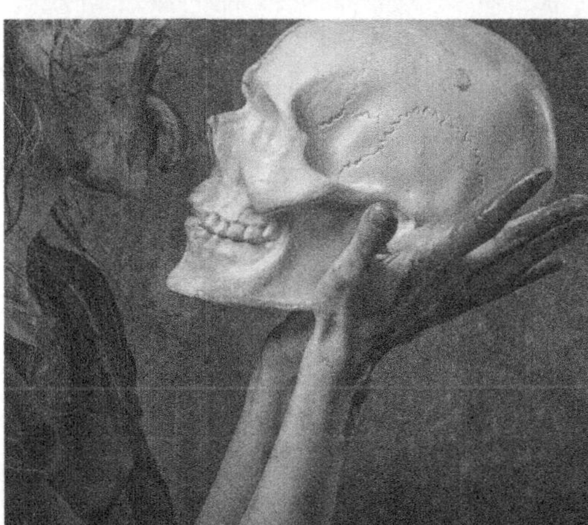

SUBMISSION CALL: "UNDEAD LOVERS" EDITED BY SYLVESTER BARZEY

WHAT DOES IT MEAN TO BE ALIVE? TO BE DEAD? TO BE neither? to be *both*? For this submission call, we're asking you to consider what it means to straddle the line between life and death, the physical and the spiritual, and the intersection of love and (blood)lust. We invite authors to reimagine what it means to be "undead" and to explore the unconventional areas of eroticism that come with it.

We're looking for stories between 1000 to 4000 words (firm) and are open to all subgenres of horror, including creature features. However, while stories about vampires, zombies, and ghosts will be considered for publication, we strongly encourage writers to think outside of the box when reimagining these classic monsters. Additionally, we welcome submissions that involve creative and more liberal interpretations of this anthology's central theme.

Please note that while a portion of *Undead Lovers* will be from invited contributors, Hedone Books is dedicated to encouraging and elevating new voices in the community. For this reason, we are pledging that at least 70% of the anthology's total word count come from unsolicited submissions.

What we would love to see: We want horror and sex that's dripping with tension. Give us work that explores characters at their breaking points, tenuous relationships, the weight of words left unspoken, and the consequences of not letting go. Send us work brimming with grief, pain, need, and regret. As this anthology features erotic horror, we encourage authors to lean into the visceral and consider ways of grounding their work in vivid tactile descriptions. Works we love include *Tender Is The Flesh* by Agustina Bazterrica, *Deadgirl* (2008), *Return Of The Living Dead 3* (1993), *Mexican Gothic* by Silvia Moreno-Garcia, *Brother* by Ania Ahlborn, and *Secrets Of A Side Bitch* by Jessica N. Watkins. For more resources on what we're looking for, be sure to check out Hedone Books on social media (under the handle @HedoneBooks) and view our pinned posts.

What we don't want: Rape fantasies, beastiality, works promoting hateful ideologies, and stories including sexual content with minors. Please note that consensual non-consent (CNC) is okay as long as it is clear it is *consensual* non-consent.

Submission period: October 1 - November 30, 2024

Length: 1,500 - 4,000 words (firm)

Payment: $0.01 USD per word

Format: Stories should be formatted in 12 pt. Times New Roman, double spaced. Please include your pen name and author email address, but do not include your phone number or address. Please include trigger warnings at the top of the page.

Rights: Exclusive First Worldwide Publication, Print and Electronic Rights for one year (from date of publication), and non-exclusive rights thereafter.

Contributor copies: One physical copy and one digital copy.

Simultaneous submissions: Allowed, but please promptly withdraw your story if it is accepted elsewhere. No reprints or multiple submissions.

Contact: All submissions should be sent to submissions@hedonebooks.com. (Word files only. Please do not paste your story in the body of the email.) Please make your subject line: UNDEAD LOVERS – "Story Title" – Author Name – Word Count.

Responses: We aim to finalize the table of contents by March 1, 2025.

Shelley Lavigne

LA PETITE MORT

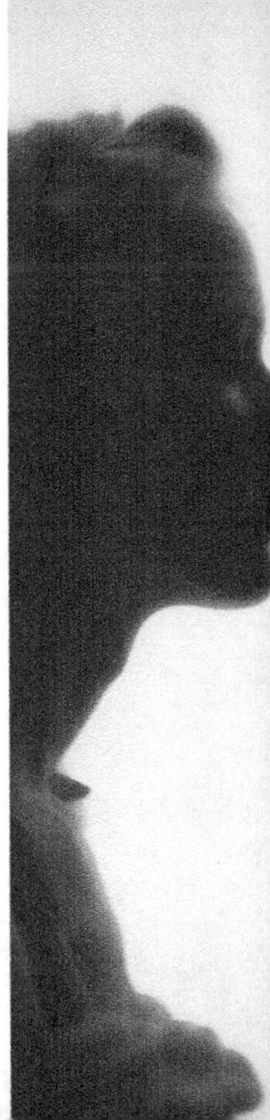

LA PETITE MORT

My breath swirled before me, a creamy ectoplasm drifting into the hallway ahead of my body. The candle flickered and I hurried to cup the flame. I did not want to be submerged in darkness, not in this old manor where shadows moaned and floors shifted beneath unseen feet.

After Claudine's séance, it was hard to dismiss the sounds as products of a settling house. The rapping yes/no answers to our questions showed intimate knowledge of our private matters—"How did it know where I hid Justine's necklace?" our former school friend Anne-Marie asked when the raps correctly identified its hiding place: a hollowed-out bible filled with pilfered treasures.

I was terrified of what it might reveal next—I had a large secret stored deep in a compartment of my hollowed-out heart, one I'd never shared with anyone.

"I heard about a medium who was taken over by the spirit of a husband whose wife was attending the séance," our other friend Lucie said.

The three of us turned to Claudine, our medium and my dearest friend. One legend turned our silly game much more dangerous.

"What happened to her?" Anne-Marie asked.

"The ghost wasn't going to dismiss himself. I heard the medium moved in with the widow and never left."

The thought of Claudine being puppeted by some malevolent ghost terrified me.

"Dismiss it, please," I begged.

She did so with a sigh and a brush of her hand, but I still felt it in every darkened corner and mysterious thump.

Sleeping alone was dangerous under those circumstances.

And maybe, *maybe* I was using that as an excuse.

But the *tick tick tick* of the grandfather clock downstairs served to remind me of the dwindling time remaining before Claudine was packed up and shipped to France, where she'd be enchanted by the salons and cafes and I'd be a distant memory, a road contemplated but never taken. Meanwhile, I'd stay stuck in Québec, ruminating over our finishing school days and the tense week we shared in this palatial home ahead of her departure. I would torture myself recalling the brush of her cold fingers on my wrists, the press of her palm on my back, the blown kiss on the nape of my neck, her toes caressing the dip of my ankle as we ate dinner.

Every time I felt the brush of her, my heart would beat out of my chest, and once I'd composed myself enough to respond, she'd already be across the room or distracted by some other activity.

The clock chimed twelve times.

The day had come. And with it, my last chance to confess.

I ran on the balls of my feet, praying that Lucie and Anne Marie were sleeping soundly—they'd snuck off giggling earlier and might be otherwise occupied.

I could smell Claudine's sweet bouquet of cherries and citrus through her door. It reminded me of cocktails we'd had after sneaking out of school to visit the hidden bar where women wore moustaches and men danced with men.

It was there she'd taught me to dance, chest to chest, in the packed room, where the walls leaned in just like we did, trying to be heard above the music. Where I felt, for one moment, that I could do it—I could kiss her. That I could take the leap and lick the bead of sweat that dangled from her earlobe—the most precious diamond in the world.

But the drink had gone to my head, and the swarm of fear and anticipation was so overwhelming, I lost my grip on consciousness. Some tiny creature of undetermined gender brought me back, waving smelling salts beneath my nose. I'd been too embarrassed to speak to Claudine for a week after, pleading to some—any—higher power that she'd forget.

That same panic gripped me again as I swirled in her scent.

My closest friend. My truest friend. How could I risk ruining this?

Creak.

I peered into the hall's darkness beyond the candle's weak light.

Creak.

The second footstep was closer.

Stomp.

I could just make out some darkened shape—

Stomp.

—Coming closer.

Stompstompstomp.

I didn't bother knocking. Throwing the door open, I ducked inside, breathing again only once my back was firmly pressed against the other side of it. Inside Claudine's bedroom.

"Berthe?" she asked, blinking in the candlelight.

"Sorry there was ... there was someone in the ... hall. A ghost?"

She peeled open her sheets and a wave of her smell, concentrated, distilled, warmed by her skin, struck me. I wanted to rub myself in it, forever be marked by her fragrance.

"Hurry up before all the heat goes out," she urged, her voice sleepy soft.

I put the candlestick on her bedside table and slipped in.

"Blow out the light, would you?"

I did, after allowing myself one last glance at her thick black curls, matted and splayed wantonly across her pillowcase. She opened her eyes, granting me a view of absinthe green irises that had the same effect on me as the liquor itself.

In the darkness, the rainstorm outside sounded even louder.

I wished I was the house and the rain were her fingers, trailing down my every surface.

Her heat was a lingering echo in the space I occupied. But I was keenly aware of that barrier between us, the resistance in that hand-span distance that seemed to push me away whenever I got too close.

"Get spooked, did you?" she asked.

"That was entirely your fault. Did you do that séance tonight just to drive me to your bed?"

We both laughed and I could picture her wry smile, the dimple that dented her right cheek. She rustled the sheets, settling in, and I tried to think of how to confess my affection to her. I'd had years to practise, but faced with a golden opportunity—my last chance—every last word failed me.

Her breathing slowed, deepening as she was taken over by sleep.

Tears of frustration filled my eyes. My last chance: gone, blown out like a candle's flame.

A low moan curled out of the darkness.

The ghost had followed me.

I ducked under the blankets, searching for cover.

Claudine shifted in the bed, pulling down my flimsy armour.

"Was that what you're scared of? It doesn't sound particularly scary."

It hadn't, no. It sounded like the moans I muffled with a pillow when imagining Claudine's hands caressing my body. The one that had ripped free of me that first night we shared a bed and woke up tangled in each other, when for a few glorious minutes there'd been nothing between us but cotton. But then discomfort—a sensation I'd once blamed on guilt—squeezed by innards and I'd rolled away. Until daybreak, we'd done no more than lay side by side and pretended to fall asleep.

I refused to repeat that experience. I couldn't. I was glad for the darkness in that moment, so she should not see my splotchy colouring, my embarrassed flush, made all the more visible by my fairness.

"Do you think ghosts fantasize like we do?" I asked.

There was a sound of skin rubbing on cotton. A nod. "Yes, what else is there to do after death?"

"What do you think they picture when they reach between their legs?"

I heard her lips part, the soft pop as they opened to her tongue. The gentle rub of it over her lips.

Thumpthumpthumpthump. I couldn't tell if that was my heart or footsteps in the hall.

"I'd much rather hear what you think," she said after a moment.

The cold brush of a toe sent gooseflesh up my leg. Panic squeezed my heart.

"I suppose they fantasize just like we do."

She chuckled, low. "Oh, come on. You can do better than that."

Her teasing dropped straight to the pit of my stomach. I clutched the sheets to prevent my hands from sliding between my legs.

"I—I ... "

"Tell me what you picture when you hear them. The moans."

I opened myself up, like she did before a séance, opened that door within my chest, let myself see without seeing. It came to me in a flood.

"I see a ghost long since dead," I said. "A creature as out of time in death as in life, cursed to wander the halls where they once lived. And I see a beautiful girl occupying the very place the ghost did in life. The ghost cannot help but watch her; what else is there to do in an existence deprived of taste, of smells, of dreams? Out of all the past occupants of the home, the girl is the sweetest—kind, meek, and much too easily exploited by the others in the ghost's house. Too frightened to name what she wants, to seize life while she has it. The girl is barely more than a ghost herself."

I felt Claudine shift, turning to face me even though we were no more visible to each other than ink stains across a starless sky.

"Years pass in this fashion. The girl becomes a woman, deemed maiden, ready to be plucked by the highest bidder. The suitors come and go and the woman remains silent, unmoved. She is reminded that if she does not make her choice, her father will on her behalf, and she simply shrugs.

"None of them are what she wants."

"What she wants has been creeping in the shadows, watching her every step, because yes, of course she knows the ghost is watching and yearning to make contact. So, on a full moon, skin silvered by light, she pleads with the ghost to reveal itself. Some power in the stars hears her plea and takes pity; she shares a little of her light with the now-illumed ghost. Never before has the woman seen someone so beautiful, and the sight brings her to tears."

A cold hand settled on my stomach, rubbing circles into the soft flesh at my middle. My breath caught on the fingertips.

"Yes?" Claudine urged me to continue.

"The woman could see the ghost, hear its voice—though faint, like wind caressing leaves. But they could not touch. Their hands pierced through each other's forms without contact.

"The woman consulted every touring medium, wrote to Spiritualists at home and abroad, but while they demanded exorbitant amounts, none of their rituals could grant the ghos

corporeality. And while the woman's power grew, while her talents as a medium became unmatched, still, in this way, she could find no solution. They could only touch in dreams, the ghost guiding the woman through the realm of the unconscious by whispering in her sleeping ear. They licked the dew from each other's skin in iridescent meadows, they played teacher and misbehaving student at a boarding school, they kissed as the world around them burned."

The hand travelled along the ridge between my breast and stomach, slowly back and forth like an aimless wanderer. I squeezed my legs together, begging for a friction I could not find.

"You were just getting to the good part," Claudine's voice was in my ear, so much closer than I thought. Her hot breath tickled my neck.

"There—there was an account—a letter—that was sent to her." It was hard to keep my breath level enough to go on. "A spiritualist had almost drowned and as she neared death, she felt the hands of a ghost pulling her back to shore. Thus, she learned that one needed to brush against the veil for the hands of the dead to make contact. Finally, she knew how to touch her soul-bound lover; she'd need to find a way to glimpse the other side, to touch death, but survive.

"The ghost had grown up with siblings—the kind who played rough—who'd discovered that cutting off air supply could invoke strange hallucinations and a pleasurable floating sensation. The kind of death was short in duration, coming back to was no more difficult than waking from a dream. This was their solution. The woman agreed, too excited at the prospect of entwining her own fingers in her lover's hands, to imagine death if things went wrong."

Another hand joined the first, this one grasping my thigh. I hissed at the cold, at the way the icy digits dug deep into my flesh. Too deep, as if to pierce me. Claudine moaned into my hair, moving closer.

I uncurled my fingers from the sheets and found her warm navel. She shuddered under my touch, shuffling closer. As I drifted lower, the hand on my thigh drifted up. I could smell our desire, the sweaty salt of it. Goosebumps pebbled my flesh.

I wanted to abandon my exploration of her body and guide her hand where I yearned for it, but this ought to be about our mutual joining, not my selfish release after years of pining.

"They tried that night. The woman had been too excited to eat supper, praying for the meal to end so that the night would come. When she was dismissed, she practically ran from the table despite her father's calls for decorum. She stripped herself bare on the threshold of her room, not even waiting for the door to close.

"She laid on her bed, nothing but the fire's heat and the ghost's burning gaze on her skin. The ghost reached down, fingers hovering above her living flesh. The woman reached up, wrapping her long fingers around her own neck. Pressing. Pressing. The ghost crept closer. The woman squeezed harder. She couldn't wait any longer. Four years had been enough. She pressed. Spots appeared in the darkness behind her eyes. Pleasure replaced her breath. Over her skin, warm pinpricks spread, like stepping into a hot bath after a cold day."

My fingers found Claudine's molten core—fire where fingers were ice—and she bucked into my hand, squeezing her legs shut and pinning me in place. Her wetness soaked through the cotton gown between us, taunting me to pull the cloth up so I could touch the silky skin between her legs.

"Keep going," she panted.

"The ghost reached out to her ... hovering fingers over her skin ... waiting for the moment when the light ... when the woman came close enough to touch ... stars danced in her eyes ... a whole world ... the ghost lowered their hands ... the woman finally felt the calluses of their rough fingers touching her soft wet warmth and ... they were cold but so firm ... so solid ... she ground into them ... hungry for contact—"

A low howl from the corner of the room broke us apart. Someone —something was watching. We lay side by side in the darkness, like cats caught with their paws in the birdcage, blood and feathers on our lips.

My voice, when it returned, had no more substance than a wavering apparition.

"After that first contact, the woman was insatiable. She hid in her room, or in the darkened corners of the house, learning the exact pressure she needed to apply before her lover could suckle at her flesh. She grew pale, nearly a corpse, taking on the traits of that which kept her company. And she'd never been happier.

"Her father noticed the changes, noted the Spiritualist Literature his daughter studied and listened to her muttered one-sided dialogues. His daughter was growing strange, perhaps too lonely in her isolation. And he knew how to fix it. Her second cousin, a rather wealthy fellow who would inherit their home upon his death—something he felt was imminent—had recently lost his comely wife and was left raising three rather energetic children alone. A wedding between the two families would be a solution to everyone's problems."

Cold fingers found my own, clasping tightly.

"The lady locked herself in her room and wailed at the ghost, no longer caring what the others in the house heard. She cried for the loss of her independence, the loss of her home, but most of all the loss of her love.

"'We will find each other again,' the ghost promised. And as they wrapped their hands around their weeping lover, she felt their touch."

Claudine shifted, and I felt a tugging at my nightgown. I reached down, pulling the fabric over my head. The cold hand—how had my body not yet warmed hers?—found my thigh again, and this time did not tantalise me further. It slipped between my legs and stroked the quickening pulse there. I whimpered, to Claudine's amusement.

"So needy," she whispered in my ear.

"I've wanted this—"

"I know."

"Why didn't you say anything?"

"I needed to see if you could do it."

The cold press found my entrance, circling the rim of me.

Teasing, dipping inside, pulling out.

"Ask for it," she said.

"Please, God. Please enter me."

Claudine licked her lips. She loved being mistaken for God. With nothing but the susurration of rain and the press of the mattress against my back, maybe she was God, maybe there was nothing else in this universe but me and her and her fingers slowly pressing into me, singly, then in doubles until I was nothing but pulsing, wet heat.

"What happened to the lady?" Claudine asked.

"God, now?"

The hand retreated from between my legs and as cold as the fingers had been, it was nothing like the clammy emptiness I felt upon their departure.

"Claude," I pleaded, using her special nickname, which only I was allowed to use. "Please, Claude."

"Be a good girl, finish the story. I want to hear how it ends. Maybe you'll get a reward when you finish."

"Claude..." I whined, but my pleas fell unheeded at the king's feet, so I tried to find the thread of the story again, recalling the ghostly touch of the woman's lover. "The woman knew she could feel her phantasm's touch only when near death, and yet the woman was using none of her usual tricks to approach the veil. She must be nearing her true death."

The hand returned between my legs, and I pressed into the fingers. A solitary digit teased me, dipping in and out. I curled my fists into my thighs rather than reaching for the hand and plunging it inside me.

Claudine wouldn't like that.

"The woman wrapped her arms tight around the ghost and promised to never let go. She ran to the open window and together they flew for a couple glorious moments, the ghost feeling the kiss of wind on the woman's face before they splattered to the cobblestones below."

A ghosting breath made my nipple rise before it was drawn between teeth. I moaned as the pain blurred into pleasure, as a tongue soothed the pebbled nipple. A hand pinched the other, twisting it. I'd never thought to play with them in this way, I was a fool for having neglected this part of my self-exploration.

At least now, at least now—

"Tell me how it ends, Berthe."

Claudine's voice was far away as if I was slipping from this plane into one where only pleasure existed.

"Their mangled souls pierced through the veil and now they're forever intertwined, forever re-living the painful ecstasy of their conjoined death."

"Close enough," Claudine said. And ripped the covers off of me.

A face nudged my legs open, a tongue replacing the fingers that filled me a moment ago. I pushed into the face as the tongue dipped deeper. I pinched my nipples, twisting like I'd just learned.

"You're a quick study," Claudine said.

A sudden lightning flash illuminated the room, revealing something that was not Claudine between my legs. Where I'd imagine Claudine was a vaporous shadow, the soot of a candle taken form.

I screamed, sitting up and scrambling back, my head hitting the carved wooden headboard hard enough to create stars.

"Shh, no, it's okay," Claudine said, stroking my face and wiping the tears that ran from my eyes.

"What's happening?"

"Well, you got some details wrong, but you were right about ghosts."

I pushed her away, or tried to, but she'd always been much stronger than me, handily beating me at tennis, beating everyone, even the instructor. Her arms kept me pressed into her very living, very real heat.

"Will you calm down?" Claudine tutted, rubbing my back. "Good girl. I needed to test whether you could connect to my spectre."

"Your ..." I couldn't bring myself to finish the sentence. To acknowledge the swirling darkness I'd glimpsed in the flash of lightning. Surrounded by Claudine's living warmth, I scolded myself for being so foolish to believe that those icy hands had belonged to anything but the dead.

But the hungry will believe anything is food, and I had been starved for Claudine since I first saw her.

"You got some details of the story right, some wrong. It wasn't a fall, it was a drowning. My father had been in the navy, he brought me back. I spent enough time over there to learn a few tricks. Like how to bind a soul to me."

"The ghost has been with you all this time?"

So much made sense, the resistance when I drew close, the fainting spell when I'd danced with her.

Claudine laughed.

"They can get a little jealous, especially when a pretty girl like you has a crush on me. But over time, they came to understand. We just wondered if you had the bravery to join us."

"Join?"

Claudine's hand, so warm and large, found mine. I was nearly swallowed by her. I wanted to be swallowed, I wanted nothing more than to crawl inside her and never leave. Ghost be damned, she would be mine.

"I can't leave you here; I can't possibly go to France without you."

"I tried, I asked, my father can't—"

"I know, but there are other ways."

A cold hand stroked my thigh. It felt good, in spite of myself, a balm for the fire that burned below my navel.

A cold hand stroked my thigh. It felt good, in spite of myself, a balm for the fire that burned below my navel.

"Don't you want to make sure we're never parted?" Claudine whispered in my ear.

"I—"

"Didn't you once tell me, when we drank the absinthe, that you'd rather die than be separated?"

"I—" I couldn't be sure, but that did sound like me.

"I don't want to be separated from you either."

The shadow hand found my centre again and I lifted my hips into it, finding friction that shouldn't exist between apparition and animate.

"Let them in, Berthe," Claudine whispered in my ear, guiding my legs apart.

I gasped as the fingers entered me again, as they pressed coldly into a place that shot lightning through my body. Claudine gently laid me out on the bed, kissing every last inch of shivering skin. The cold tongue sucked at my dimpled thigh one moment, biting into me in the next.

"Perfect, you're so perfect."

I preened under her affirmations, blushing at her praise.

The ghostly fingers picked up their pace inside me and my heart followed their rhythm. I begged for more, more fullness, more speed, more pressure. The hands obliged and too much became not enough and I took my own pleasure as Claudine whispered encouragement into my neck, licking the sweat from the cup of my collarbone. I could feel myself getting close, the toe-curling waves of pleasure starting to spread from my centre, building, stoked by the finger of the ghostly hand.

"Not yet," Claudine warned.

I whimpered and was pinched for my insolence.

"My turn," Claudine said from the foot of the bed. The ghost made way for warm flesh. Claudine trained her hands from my toes all the way up my legs before placing a kiss below my navel. I chased her mouth with my hips.

"I should call you Needy," Claudine said.

"Call me what you want, but please stop teasing."

Her hot breath grazed my second lips as she laughed, tongue flicking slowly along the curve of my hip.

The ghost straddled my stomach, forcing pressure against my impulses, keeping me from pushing into Claudine's face.

"Cheater," I hissed at it, low enough that Claudine wouldn't hear.

A cold tongue found my right nipple, then my left, and I wondered for a moment if I hadn't been too harsh. If I shouldn't learn to share as the ghost had.

Two cold hands wrapped themselves around my throat and squeezed. Starbursts of light tore the universe open before me, filling my vision.

"Okay, you can let go." Claudine nestled her head between my legs. Finally after all this time. She was warm, so warm, like the sun.

Cold lips pressed themselves to mine and pushed air between my parted lips and I let myself fly out of my own body in a burst of starlight. Waves of pure incandescence coursed through me, pure unfiltered pleasure. It would have gone on for eternity if a cry hadn't brought me back to reality.

Hovering, weightless, I was aware of the distance between me and the bed, me and Claudine. I watched in silence as she embraced the ghost that now wore my skin. As she kissed what had once been my lips. Hands that had once been mine felt my face, dipping between my lips to caress my teeth, press at my nose, my neck, breasts... My former eyes burst into tears which Claudine kissed away.

"It's done," she whispered, "we've finally done it."

I wailed, flying down at the reclined shapes. But my fingers slipped through flesh I could not damage, and failed to grasp at hair I wanted to pull. I did no more than raise gooseflesh with my rage.

Claudine hushed me, as cold as the ghostly fingers had been. "Think this through, do you not love me enough to share?"

I roared. "Give me back my body!" But it was futile. I had been chosen for a reason, cultivated for this. Groomed for years. Teased and led along on a leash of shared secrets and held eye contact. Hinted promises, always held just out of reach. I was never going to defeat her true paramour. I'd only ever been good at cowering, good at following orders.

"If you do not settle, I will have no choice but to dismiss you."

She turned back to the spectre wearing my skin and let her hand trail between my legs. False me moaned, looking up into my eyes as I screeched, bed frame rattling under my assault.

"I'd hoped you could share. Pity," Claudine said, waving me away with sticky fingers.

Like a curl of candle smoke, I dissipated into the void.

SHELLEY LAVIGNE

"ENAMOURED: A NOVELLA IN FRAGMENTS"

After a gorgeous socialite enters Josephine Walker's apothecary, she'll do anything to make her a regular customer, including treating her with an experimental procedure called Enameling. But when her client's desire for perfection goes too far, Josephine is forced to flee—with her client's corpse and jewels in tow. Told through an interconnected set of stories, Josephine defies the world's rigid gender expectations to take control of her life in this sapphic tale of erotic, cosmetic horror.

Shelley Lavigne is a purveyor of moist literature, usually queer oddities. They live in Ontario where they roam their neighbourhood in search of haunted houses and cool bugs. Their novella *The Flesh of the Sea*, co-authored with Lor Gislason, will be out Summer 2024 through Dark Lit Press. You can also find them online at shelleylavigne.com

A CHAT WITH

Z. K. Abraham

A CHAT WITH Z. K. ABRAHAM

Z. K. ABRAHAM (SHE/HER) IS A WRITER AND PSYCHIATRIST. SHE has been published in *Clarkesworld*, *The Rumpus*, *Fantasy Magazine*, *FIYAH Magazine*, *JMWW*, and more. She will be a Royal Literary Fund Reading Round lector for 2024-2025. She is represented by Carleen Geisler at ArtHouse Literary Agency.

The Hedone editorial team had a chance to sit down and talk with Abraham about her writing, her love of horror, and her upcoming anthology with Hedone Books, *Silk and Foxglove*.

THANK YOU SO MUCH FOR TAKING THE TIME TO TALK TO US at Hedone Books! You have an impressive bibliography to your name. Which of your works are you most proud of? Or are there any that have a special meaning to you?

Thank you for asking, I'm so glad to be a part of the Hedone Books family! I've published short stories in various genres, from literary to science fiction to fantasy, and am particularly proud of a few flash pieces published recently. One is a literary autofiction piece entitled

"The Basket" in *JMWW*. That piece came out in one draft, with a nice back and forth rhythm from past to present. Another piece is a very weird, body horror/sensory mind-fuck involving one woman's obsession with macaroni and cheese; it's called, "Kraft" and was published by *hex literary*. My favorite pieces tend to be either my quietest or most horrifying. I have a lightly speculative, deeply personal piece coming out in *Fractured Literary* called "The Unction," in which I reflected on how children deal with dislocation from their immigrant identities as well as coping with aging parents and their needs. In this story, I have the adult children trying to relearn their culture's magic, to try and heal their ailing parent. Finally, I am so proud to have a dark, reflective, science fiction piece published in *Clarkesworld*—this story took a lot of re-writing and digging to figure out. I enjoyed how the piece explored the self vs machine, past vs future, individualism vs collectivism. I also think it's an example of how I edited a piece to be more cohesive, and where I could still improve and continue to grow.

What do you feel is the main source of inspiration for your fiction? Are there any themes, character archetypes, or personal experiences that you find constantly informing your work?

I'm drawn to themes around identity, non-Western cultural backgrounds, and personal explorations of meaning in an overwhelming, dissociated world. I often write characters like myself (though I swear I want to expand beyond that!) and I have found it therapeutic to use speculative themes to convey my experiences with my queerness, my East African background, and my own anxieties. Common themes include breaking away from–yet reconciling with–traditional expectations, overbearing parental figures, obsessive productivity, fear of vulnerability. I love a character getting infected by a demonic force, obsession, body horror, sensual and sensory details.

. . .

What are some genres you're hoping to explore through your writing? Any formats or mediums you're hoping to try your hand at in the near(ish) future?

Right now, I'm very excited about "literary horror." I've been watching more horror films, reading elevated horror books. I enjoy the possibilities in horror for psychological exploration, visceral sensory details, sensuality, and terror. I hope to write more literary horror novels (in fact, I'm finishing a new draft right now). I am also interested in: writing a straightforward literary novel, an essay collection/memoir combining criticism and personal experience, a dark comedy novel, a screenplay, and also potentially trying to do performance art!

Who are some of your favourite literary influences?

I have been influenced in recent years by Rumaan Alam's *Leave the World Behind*, the psychological explorations and dread of Shirley Jackson's work, and the eco-horror of *Annihilation* by Jeff Vandermeer.

We at Hedone Books are extremely excited to be working with you on the upcoming eco-eroticism anthology, *Silk and Foxglove*, that's planned for 2025. What drew you to the idea?

I love the immense potential of eco-eroticism for authors to play with the *physical*. Nature contains uncontrolled growth as well as decay, and offers tactile experiences when we walk outside, touch earth, leaves, bark, feel temperature, smell flowers and wet soil. Nature has lots of dark unknowns. There are so many possible ways to explore the body's interaction with nature through eco-horror. I'd argue that nature is inherently erotic.

. . .

What is it about nature that you think pairs well with horror and erotica?

Poets like Wordsworth were in awe of nature, and held "transcendentalist" beliefs that nature and man were intimately connected through a divine power. They also loved the idea of the "sublime," which could be inspired by nature. The sublime is an experience, perhaps while witnessing nature's power or grandeur, that contains intense passion, awe, as well as terror. Outside of Western traditions, many Indigenous cultures have a different understanding of and respect for our intimate connections to nature. A landscape can help as well as hinder; storms, predators, and harsh, unforgiving terrain can be used in different ways to create atmosphere and tension.

What are some of your favourite eco-horror or eco-erotic works that you encourage authors check out to get a better idea of what you're looking for?

I would recommend Jeff Vandmeer's work, *The Seep* by Chana Porter, *Fever Dream* by Samanta Schweblin, and as a bonus,

Entangled by Merlin Sheldrake.

When it comes to this submission call, what are some of the things that you're hoping to see in the stories for consideration? What's on your manuscript wishlist, so to speak?

I'm hoping for plants coming to life and growing over bodies, for explorations of the darkest corners of forests, for folk horror, for myths and legends around nature from non-Western cultures, climate change metaphors, nature as dominant, visceral, and dream-like. I'm a huge fan of body horror, so anything that fits those themes will catch my eye!

Is there any final advice you'd like to give

prospective authors ahead of sending work to this submission call?

I would suggest authors lean into the physicality and sensory details of their stories, but not forget to maintain the tension central to horror. With respect to body horror, I enjoy the sensual combined with the grotesque.

THANK YOU SO MUCH AGAIN FOR TAKING THE TIME TO speak with us! Can you let everyone know where to find you, and your work, online?

You can find me at my website, zkabraham.com, infrequently on twitter with the handle @pegasusunder1, and on bluesky with the username @pegasusunder.

Z. K. ABRAHAM

"SILK AND FOXGLOVE"

Z. K. Abraham (she/her) is a writer and psychiatrist. She has been published in *Clarkesworld*, *Fractured Lit*, *The Rumpus*, *Fantasy Magazine*, FIYAH *Magazine*, JMWW, and more. She is a Royal Literary Fund Reading Round lector for 2024-2025. She is represented by Carleen Geisler at ArtHouse Literary Agency.

Submission Call

SILK AND FOXGLOVE

edited by

Z. K. Abraham

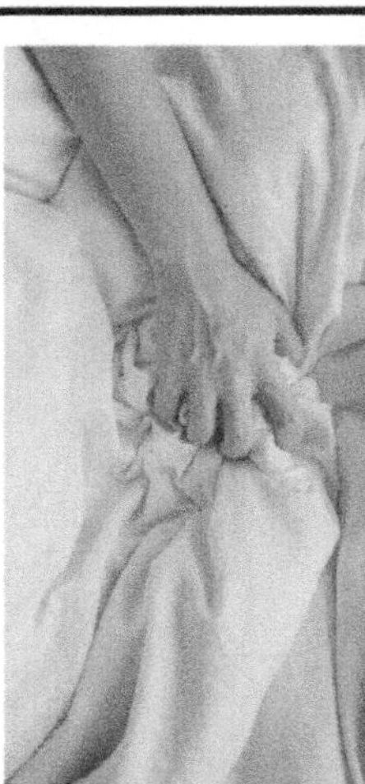

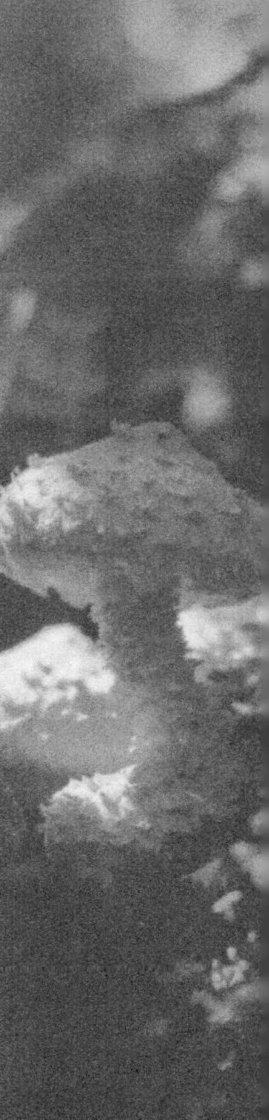

SUBMISSION CALL: "SILK AND FOXGLOVE" EDITED BY Z. K. ABRAHAM

ECO-HORROR EXPLORES THE IDEA OF NATURE BECOMING THE source of terror; in an article for MUBI, Danielle Burgos describes eco-horror as "nature becomes *uncanny* and *maliciously turned against man.*" In a *Teen Vogue* article "Ecosexuals are Queering Environmentalism," musician Peaches describes Mother Earth as a lover. "Sex-ecologist" Annie Sprinkle amusingly reflects on how "all this wood here is very sensual." Ecosexuality might include, "masturbating with water pressure, using eco-friendly lubricant, or literally having sex with a tree."

Nature as setting or character contains so much possibility for the sensual and horrifying. Nature is inherently physical and erotic; we are stripped down to our most grounded, raw selves in nature. We can experience the tactile and sensual when we touch plants, bark, earth, when we smell flowers, when we feel the shift in temperature or moisture in the air. However, nature contains decay as well as growth. Shadows move between distant trees, while legends and folktales come to life in forests and valleys and deserts. In nature's beauty, there is a sense of power beyond our grasp, an awe-inspiring terror, as well as a delicate intimacy.

With this anthology, we are looking for stories between 1500 to 4000 words (firm) that explore eco-horror with a sexy or erotic spin. Please note that for this call, we will only be considering submissions from BIPOC authors. Additionally, while a portion of the anthology will be from invited contributors, Hedone Books is dedicated to encouraging and elevating new voices in the community. For this reason, we are pledging that at least 70% of the anthology's total word count come from unsolicited submissions.

WHAT WE WOULD LOVE TO SEE: IN OUR ANTHOLOGY, WE ARE looking for the tactile, the mysterious, the terrifying and the erotic. We want seductive flowers, threatening plants, leaves caressing flesh, the dark corners of forests, folk horror, myths and legends from non-Western cultures, queerness, anti-colonialism, breaking away from the imposed shame of Western cultures on the body and nature, climate change metaphors and nature's revenge, nature as dominant, body horror, the visceral and the dream-like. We are inspired by work from Jeff Vandermeer, Chana Porter, Samantha Schweblin, Tiffany Morris, Hedone's very own Caitlin Marceau and Lindz McLeod, and more. We love movies from *Midsommar* to a one minute eco-erotic video-poem of "Night Rain" by Tania Haberland and directed by Poetics of Reverie. For more resources on eco-eroticism and what we're looking for, be sure to check out Hedone Books on social media (under the handle @HedoneBooks) and view our pinned posts.

WHAT WE DON'T WANT: RAPE FANTASIES, BEASTIALITY, works promoting hateful ideologies, and stories including sexual content with minors. Please note that consensual non-consent (CNC) is okay as long as it is clear it is consensual non-consent.

. . .

Submission period: August 1 - September 30, 2024

Length: 1,500 - 4,000 words (firm)

Payment: $0.01 USD per word

Format: Stories should be formatted in 12 pt. Times New Roman, double spaced. Please include your pen name and author email address, but do not include your phone number or address. Please include trigger warnings at the top of the page.

Rights: Exclusive First Worldwide Publication, Print and Electronic Rights for one year (from date of publication), and non-exclusive rights thereafter.

Contributor copies: One physical copy and one digital copy.

Simultaneous submissions: Allowed, but please promptly withdraw your story if it is accepted elsewhere. No reprints or multiple submissions.

Contact: All submissions should be sent to submissions@hedonebooks.com. (Word files only. Please do not paste your story in the body of the email.) Please make your subject line: SILK AND FOXGLOVE – "Story Title" – Author Name – Word Count.

. . .

Responses: We aim to finalize the table of contents by December 1, 2024.

LB Waltz

THE REDAMANCY

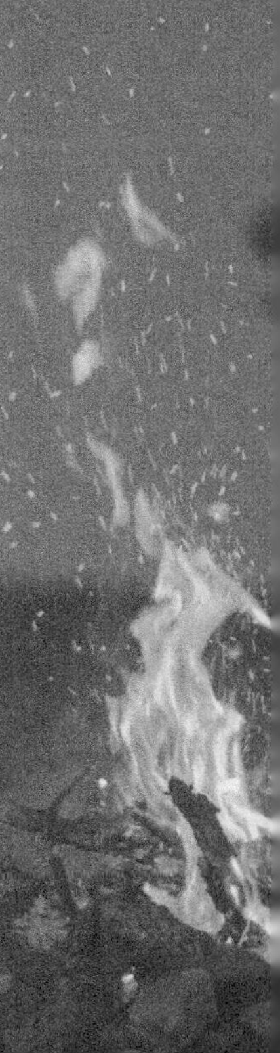

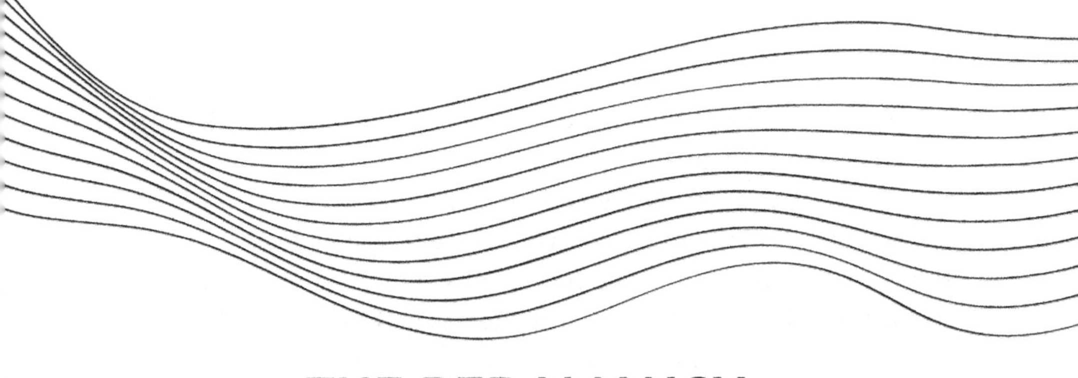

THE REDAMANCY

6.

He is kept in a little red room.

Kept. That's the word. Not *lives,* not *stays*, not even *sleeps,* because when it comes to stating truths, Ethan isn't as fulsome as his favorite authors, nor as sanguine as the Redamancy's whores.

He is kept. Like a pet would be, or a toy in a box—taken out when his aunt wishes to play and shut away when she doesn't.

And ay, there's the rub, the boy grouses, turning a page. The cheeks framing his scowl are already the same ruddy shade as the wallpaper; they darken the longer he stews in old grievances. On bitter consequences.

On his windows.

It has been one month since their initial boarding, but Ethan is still seeing red. Angry, bleeding, *literal* red. Rather than ease his loss, time accentuates it. Ethan misses the drab city skies as others might miss a lover or a limb. Oh, he misses *color*. The gray-green bustles, the off-brown suit coats. The shadows of people and shops and carriages. Every dark smear streaked across the rain-dappled glass was to the boy the stuff of rainbows, bright and magical, and he fears he will go mad with the want of them.

Perhaps that process has already begun.

Beneath the buttons of his waistcoat and the cotton of his shirt-front, Ethan's chest blisters in the heat of so much suppressed emotion. Its fires burn hotter and hotter until there is nothing left inside him but a smoldering, scarlet numbness.

A smoldering, scarlet, spreading numbness.

What will happen when that tingle creeps outward, upward, into his head? He has read of prisoners losing their minds: victims to claustrophobia, or paranoia, or rats. Certainly, they would nibble through sanity with the same ease as flesh. Hell, those vermin may need to do nothing more drastic than draw blood.

That is where lunacy begins, they say. In the blood.

Stop it.

Violently, Ethan turns another page, fingers shaking. His head mimics the motion. *No.*

No, I am not thinking about that. I am not thinking about her. That's what she wants. I refuse to do what she wants.

But being raised to do just that, he does so all the same, powerless against the subtle manipulation of his own intrusive thoughts. Damn it all, but he cannot hide from what is already inside his head. He cannot even close his eyes to it. The gloom behind his lids can offer no reprieve when there are gas lamps shining through his veins, illuminating his memories like magic lantern slides.

Flesh, decor, his own flickering recall. All glows a gory *red.*

"*And that's fitting,*" says Aunt Alice's voice in his ear. In his mind. He hears her echo in his skull, her croons resonating through time and space, from elevens to now. "*Red is the color of love, my dear. What better decorations could there be for the home of one's precious nephew?*"

In answer, Ethan had dunked a biscuit in his tea. "*Shackles?*"

"*Tosh. You are a treasure—all that I do is to protect you. How else does one guard a treasure, if not under lock and key?*"

"*You could always take me to the beach,*" Ethan countered, avoiding her gaze by glowering at his own visage in a spoon. The distortion of his features in its bowl reminded him of puberty, an observation that left him feeling even more uncomfortable. "*Bring me out to sea. Put me in a little box and drown me. Like a pirate would. No one would find me in Davy Jones's Locker, either. And I'd appreciate the change in scenery.*"

Sunken leaves floated cadaverously in the shallow depths of the drink. Hot water burbled. Bled. With finality, his aunt placed her cup upon its saucer, her ruby rings set a-twinkle by the candelabrums' haze, and repeated, "*This is fitting. This fits you, and you fit here.*"

Then her smile climbed so far up her face that the paint on her

lips could have smudged beneath her eyes. Garbed in carmine silks and wine-colored lace, Aunt Alice looked like a floating head in front of the wallpaper, her powdered profile framed by auburn curls.

A morbid contrast. Even now, Ethan's bowels twist at the thought of it.

Like a decapitated corpse. Like the remnants of a sacrifice. Like a...

He does not like to think about it. He does not want to think about it. Which— obviously—means that Ethan can think of nothing else, no matter how hard he tries to focus on his books. Between the madness that he feels and the madness that he suspects, there is no helping it; white paper, black ink, his pressed flower bookmark—everything he's read becomes exactly that in his mind's eye.

Red.

This fits you, and you fit here. Said with a smile. Said with that *smile. This is fitting.* He *fits* here. He fits *here*, in the Redamancy. In its arterial halls and chambers. In the great, beating heart of the city's most distinctive house of pleasure.

It is my home. Our home.

Ethan is attuned to it. To the incessant flow in its halls, to its never-ending pulse. To the deformations and maladies and cancerous, mutated interpretations of the conventional, to the anomalies that have revealed themselves to him slowly, so slowly, over the course of pages and whispers and years and promises.

A flattened cherry sprig revolves between his fingers, its translucent petals as pale as skin.

If someone's 'normal' is abnormal, does that make him abnormal, too? Or is he instead the product of a different normalcy?

Am I an apple caught in the roots of my own family tree? Is something... wrong with me?

"Little Master?"

Ethan starts. The twig stops. And for a moment—a stuttering instant—his heart follows suit because, through the gaps in desiccated branches, there are feathers flitting. Raven's feathers.

Oh.

Flustered, the boy slots his flowers back into his novel. "What is it, Edgar?"

"The door, Little Master." Blinking, the man in delicate black considers Ethan's squirm, torn between amusement and professionalism. "Did you not hear? The others were knocking."

Were they? Possibly. Probably. Until a minute ago, Ethan's thoughts had been too loud to hear much else. Now, the silence beyond the door is similarly deafening.

"Ah. Well. I suppose I shall have to take your word on that." Preoccupied, Ethan reaches for the teacup that Edgar sets on the table beside his armchair. Fingers meet porcelain, though not as dexterously as intended; the click of a handle against its saucer resonates through the little red room, turning the boy's thoughts to needlepoint heels. Of the sound they make against the wood grain.

"If I might be so bold, sir, the other Ladies and Gentlemen have missed seeing you."

In his cup, rosehip tea swishes like the fabric of the women's trousers. It swirls like the men's gowns. Dregs settle, then darken. Ethan's mood does the same.

"Still no windows," he grumbles. Reflected eyes ripple, but return his glare. "Did you notice that, Edgar? No windows, but the bedroom door was left unlocked. Like a *compromise*." The word sour is on his tongue, enough so to curdle milk. He shoves away the china creamer. An offered sugar cube is crushed beneath his thumb. "She's done that on purpose. She knows, somehow. She must. Whenever she unlocks that damn door, that's when I feel the most..."

Trapped.

"Sir?"

Concern further softens the velvet qualities of Edgar's voice. His awful, lovely voice. Ethan's awful, lovely Edgar.

LB WALTZ

"THE REDAMANCY"

Upon coming of age in his abusive aunt's Victorian-era bordello, Ethan longs to escape the prison of his locked quarters and explore the tantalizing secrets hidden in the brothel's rooms. To sate his curiosity and desire for freedom, he seduces the only person besides his aunt who can set him free: the man who works as his servant by day and a lady by night. But some secrets can't be unlearned and the freedom Ethan longs for may just destroy him.

LB Waltz has been publishing creative works for over 20 years under various pseudonyms. They enjoy taking walks, biblically accurate depictions of angels, and reading about botanical folklore. Follow them on Twitter at @balmroomdance.

Dori Lumpkin

DON'T HANG UP THE PHONE

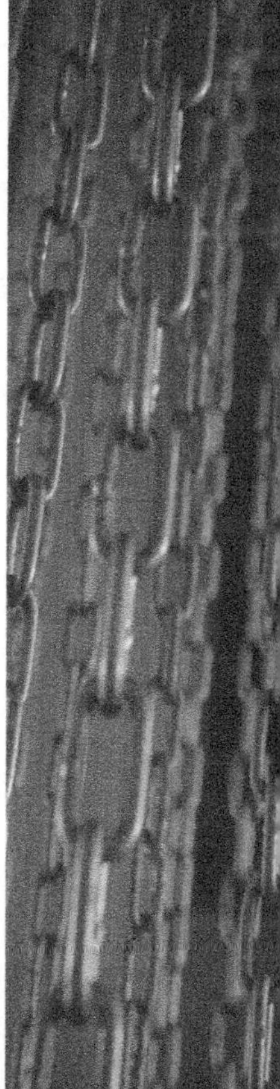

DON'T HANG UP THE PHONE

SCENE ONE

YOU'RE HOME ALONE. OF COURSE YOU ARE, YOU *HAVE* TO BE for this to work. Your roommates went out for the evening, so you've got the house to yourself. This is a rare occurrence. You thought you'd celebrate.

Your boyfriend is supposed to come over later.

You thought the two of you would snuggle up. Maybe watch a scary movie. You'd act more afraid than you actually are—he doesn't need to know. The point is, that would make him wrap his arm around you in the way that you'd been hoping he would for weeks now. One thing would lead to another, and, well... let's fade to black here. For now.

You're making popcorn.

It's good, that QuickPop stuff that comes pre-buttered. Spent the extra money on the name brand instead of whatever you'd normally buy yourself for a night like this. You got it just for tonight, didn't you? How fun.

It's a miracle none of your roommates have taken it before now, selfish assholes that they are. If your name isn't written on the top of it in huge, clearly marked letters, it must be fair game. They're like that.

They always have been. They take up space and time and whatever the fuck else they want to take up, pushing you to the edges like you don't even matter.

But you're fine. You're sweet, they say. You listen, and you talk to them, and you always forgive, because that's the kind of good, home-grown girl you are. It isn't their fault that they forgot to clean up the bathroom, or left ash all over the coffee table, even though one of the house rules is *please no smoking inside*. You swept it up without a word because you believe that people are good, and they wouldn't be taking advantage of you, because why would someone do that, right?

You're looking for new places once the lease is up, aren't you?

Thinking about moving in with that boyfriend—what's his name, Billy or Jason or Charlie or something? That would be sweet. A little home. Maybe you'll get a dog. One that eventually you'll come to think is an annoying little shit, and your boyfriend an even more annoying little shit, and you'll be so unhappy and bring yourself back to this night pretty often, wondering exactly where it all went wrong. If your roommates were right, and maybe you do need to let loose. Live a little, see what happens.

You wonder if you should have gone out with them. If you would have had a better time at a bar or a club, getting drunk and telling your boyfriend you have other plans. You wonder where they went—try to remember what they said. They wrote it down—you made them do that, just in case they needed you. You could go—

No.

You can't.

You can't take it back now, can you?

No. You're making popcorn.

It's too late for all of that.

SCENE TWO

The phone rings. You roll your eyes, annoyed. It could be one of them, drunk already and needing a ride home. You promised you'd answer if they called because you're a good roommate and an even better friend. You'd go pick them up in a heartbeat if they asked.

You abandon your popcorn, preparing your speech, getting ready to tell them that it's only been about an hour, and if they're coming home so quickly, it wasn't worth it to go out at all.

"Hello?" You say, the annoyance clear enough.

"Hello," another voice comes through. Unexpected. Lower than any of your roommates. Something about it rubs you the wrong way, but you choose to ignore it for now.

"Can I help you with something?" You say. It's in your nature to help. *How sweet.*

"I don't know," the voice replies, "can you?"

There is a certain teasing quality to it that you appreciate. It reminds you of an older brother, or maybe even your boyfriend.

"I think you have the wrong number," you say. "Who were you trying to reach?"

"I don't know," the voice responds, a smile behind it now, "why don't you tell me your name, and I'll let you know if I have the right number or not."

You roll your eyes, certain now more than ever that the person on the other end is either a roommate or a friend-of-a-roommate enlisted in some shitty prank.

"I told you guys to call me if you needed something, don't just call me to fuck with me."

You turn back to the popcorn, which has started to grow underneath the foil.

"How do you know I'm calling just to fuck with you?" You hear some rustling in the background of the call but decide not to mention it. Better to not give this weirdo more things to talk to you about.

"Because that's what you guys do. You go out, and then you call me and act like creeps, or you pretend there's been some huge disaster so that I come and help you and by the time I get there, everything is fine and you just wanted to get me out of the house."

You shuffle the popcorn on the stove, willing it to pop faster, willing your boyfriend to arrive sooner, willing this person to get over their fixation on you and end the damn call.

"Sounds like you've got some pretty shit friends," the voice says. You realize then that maybe this isn't a prank. Maybe this isn't any of your roommates, and maybe you should be a whole lot more careful about what you say to strangers on the phone.

You hesitate.

"I gotta go, actually." Your voice is stilted now. Tense. "Sorry."

"Don't hang up." There's a shift in tone that makes you nervous. An unspoken threat that causes a twist in the pit of your stomach. Your finger hovers over the button. The voice speaks again, not angry, but firm.

"*Don't hang up, or I'll slaughter you and your meathead boyfriend too.*"

SCENE THREE

You hang up. Of course you do, who wouldn't have? The person on the other end of the line overdid it, and that lost them their chance of talking to you, especially on a night as important as this one.

You check the clock.

Your boyfriend was supposed to be here by now.

Wasn't he?

Maybe the voice on the phone *was* him, trying to pull some sort of prank. Trying to scare you even more before you watch the movie together, drawing the tension out so that he can make a big deal out of "calming you down" later. He likes threats, he likes to play his little games. Totally reasonable.

You resolve to ask him when he gets there, to tell him to fuck off with that shit, and to never put you in a position like that again.

When he gets here.

Which is *when* exactly?

You check the clock again, the blinking red lights edging into danger territory. He's never been this late before. He might be irresponsible and annoying, but he could be punctual for the most part, which is one of the few things you admire about him. Other than the sorts of things that happen after we fade to black, that is.

Reaching for the phone again, you decide to give him a call. He's probably on his way; he might've gotten lost. The road up to your house is tricky–difficult to navigate in the dark. You lost track of the amount of times your roommates had asked people over, only for them to get lost and give up along the way. It was an endless source of disappointment for them, but it brought you comfort at the time. There was a sense of safety to it, being so out and alone.

Alone.

Your mind must linger on that for a moment, because a panicked look comes over your face, and your fingers scramble to dial your boyfriend's number faster than they ever have before. You slip a few times, having to redial more than once. Finally, you manage to get the whole number out, and you listen to it ring, eyeing the knives in the block on the counter.

Better safe than sorry, right?

You should defend yourself, shouldn't you?

You reach for a knife, but in the moment before you're able to grab it, the call goes through.

Voicemail.

You sigh, resolving not to let the dead phone line make you nervous. The knife remains in the block.

"Um, hey baby," you start out, "it's me. I'm just calling to make sure you're okay? It's late, and you were supposed to be here by now. I'm feeling a little..." you trail off, not really sure how to phrase what's going on, "I don't know. Anyway. Call me back. Or show up, I guess."

You hang up. You turn back to the popcorn.

Three seconds go by before you pick up the phone again and dial the same number.

It doesn't even ring this time. Straight to voicemail, like you're some sort of annoyance, something to be disregarded or forgotten.

You don't bother to leave a message this time.

You just hang up.

SCENE FOUR

It rings again, almost as soon as you set it back on the counter. You jump and then laugh at yourself for how silly this all feels. He's just calling you back! That's all. He missed your call because he was trying to find the turn, and now he's calling to let you know that he's right outside, and there's no reason to worry at all. More than ready for the relief that comes with hearing your boyfriend's voice after all of that, you click the button.

"I thought I told you not to hang up." That tinny, false-feeling male voice echoes through the speaker.

"Leave me alone or I'm calling the police." You hope the person on the other end of the line doesn't hear it for the empty threat that it is. You probably wouldn't call the police. You don't make it a habit to do that, because you don't particularly like them. But it's as good a threat as any and usually makes people leave you alone.

"Do it, then," the voice taunts. "I don't believe you."

"I have a boyfriend!" You immediately move on to your next threat, "he's big, and he's strong, and he'll beat the shit out of you!"

The voice just laughs, which sends an unsettling thrill down your spine. This has to be some sort of prank, right?

"He's late though, isn't he?"

You glance at the clock again, the red lights still blinking into oblivion. Yeah, he's late. But you aren't going to admit that.

"No," you say, and you immediately curse how awkward it sounds. "He's here, and he's got a knife."

You don't know why you add that last part. Maybe you wanted to up the threat itself? Did you want to scare the person on the other end of the line? As if that would do anything. You don't even have a knife, you didn't even grab it, and now your gaze is flickering back over to the block, and you wonder if maybe you should—

"A knife?" The voice interrupts, and it doesn't believe you. You know it doesn't believe you.

And you're scared.

It's *thrilling*.

"Well," the voice continues, "tell your big strong boyfriend to come and fuck me up then, why don't you?" They're teasing you. You know they're teasing you.

"Maybe I will," you shoot back.

"He's in the backyard. It would be so easy."

The voice goes silent, and you can't bring yourself to hang up. You call out his name—Billy or Jason or Charlie again—but get no response.

It's too easy for you to abandon the QuickPop and run to the back of the house. You don't even consider that the voice might be bluffing, might want you to move away from the front door that you definitely didn't lock.

There are lots of things that you don't consider. That you forget about. You always thought you'd be braver in a situation like this. Guess not, huh?

You flick on the back porch lights, leaving the yard awash in bright fluorescence.

SCENE FIVE

You find your boyfriend. He was here, after all. How sweet.

Based on the way he's sitting, he probably had gotten here a lot sooner than you thought but got…delayed, you'd assume.

Someone has pulled one of your iron lawn chairs—a gift from a roommate's parents upon moving in—and positioned it directly in front of the window, about fifteen feet back. In it sits your boyfriend but he doesn't exactly look comfortable. His wrists are bound to the arms of the chair with thick, dark rope, and his legs are done up in the same manner. There's a swathe of red cloth shoved into his mouth, held in place with stretches of silver tape that seem to wrap all the way around his head.

You're frozen.

Behind him, there stands a figure, dressed in one of those shitty, Halloween Grim Reaper costumes that go for fifteen dollars at any party store. You'd laugh, if the figure wasn't holding a knife right next to your boyfriend's ear, blade poised to slam through bone and cartilage and straight to the brain itself. Whatever little your boyfriend has of one, at least.

Your senses come back to you, and you move into action.

"Don't hurt him!" You shout. "Please!"

You get the sense that if you tried to go out there, you'd be as good as dead, which is a pretty decent instinct. You stay put, and watch your boyfriend's face contort, his eyes widening with fear and his body shaking with what might be sobs, or anger, or some other wasteful emotion.

"Take your clothes off, or I'll gut your boyfriend like a fucking hog. Okay, pretty?"

You've got no time for confusion. No time to wonder about the voice on the other end of the line, or the person in the mask outside, standing over Billy or Jason or Charlie with a knife. You can't consider that the figure outside doesn't even *have* a phone, and certainly couldn't know exactly what's going on inside your house, unless—

Whatever.

You'll find out eventually.

"*HEY*!" The voice shouts in your ear, and you jump again, nodding.

"Okay, okay!"

You're in your pajamas, so it isn't exactly difficult. Shaking, you push the elastic of your striped pants down, moving slowly. If things weren't so tense, someone might've accused you of putting on a show.

After your pants are discarded, you move to the buttons of your shirt, undoing them one at a time until your breasts are exposed to the cool air of your home, your boyfriend, and whoever that other person is outside. Your breath is coming in heavy bursts now, and you attempt to calm yourself by holding it for just a second. You release.

It doesn't help.

"Turn the dining chair around so that your boyfriend can see you, and take a seat."

You follow this next set of instructions, feeling more like a puppet than a person. The fabric of the seat isn't comfortable against your bare skin, but you're not exactly in a position to complain.

"Now touch yourself." Your breath catches in your throat as you realize exactly what this person wants you to do. The knife hovers over your boyfriend's skin in a treacherous reminder of what might happen if you disobey.

"You won't hurt him, right? If I do it?" Your free hand—the one not holding the phone—drifts over your legs and stomach, leaving goosebumps in its wake.

"Right," the voice responds, "that's what I said."

SCENE SIX

You do as the voice says because there's nothing else to do.

You use your free hand to move over your skin, playing carefully with the folds between your legs. You should be shocked at how wet you are, but it doesn't come as much of a surprise, really. The thrill of it makes sense. The adrenaline. Your heart rate ticks up a notch, and your boyfriend watches with wide eyes as your index finger circles your clit.

It feels good.

Too good.

You amp up the pace, breathing heavily and moving your ring finger back and forth, every so often letting it slip down slightly, just grazing over the edge of your hole.

You moan, and that *does* take you by surprise. The voice laughs.

"You can do more than that, can't you?" The voice taunts you again. "Fuck yourself."

You aren't exactly one to deny someone what they want, are you?

You nod, slipping one finger inside of yourself, using the others to continue toying with your clit, playing with your folds.

But it isn't enough.

It still doesn't feel like enough.

You slip another finger in, your ring finger joining your middle finger, and delight at the slight stretching sensation.

Yes, this is better, isn't it?

You pump your fingers in and out, grinding your hips down

against your hand as you try harder and harder to give yourself more.

"Good girl," the voice crackles through the phone. "Keep going."

Those words get you. You feel something shoot through your body, and you can't stop the moan that spills from your lips.

Tension and heat build low in your stomach as you continue to move your fingers in and out, letting your thumb brush over your clit every now and again for another jolt of pleasure. Your eyes drift shut as you do so, mouth hanging open

If anyone asked, you'd tell them you were thinking of your boyfriend in that moment. You wished it was him touching you, you wished you had gotten to watch a movie and let things fade to black.

But actually?

Pressure and pleasure spill over into completion, and you reach orgasm thinking about the knife against your boyfriend's throat, and that stupid Grim Reaper costume being the one standing over you, holding it against you, forcing you to do the things you're doing.

You come with a shout, your whole body tensing and twitching as you try to catch your breath.

Don't tell anyone, but that might've been the strongest orgasm you've ever had.

The voice comes back to you through the phone, a little out of breath as well.

"I'm going to turn the lights off, and you're going to get a surprise, okay?"

As fucked as it is, the voice sounds reassuring. Calm. Nothing you ever would have gotten from your boyfriend. You almost want to trust it.

You feel guilty almost as soon as you think it, knowing that there's nothing he can do from where he is. Pathetic little shit. He's out there, tied up like a loser, and you're giving it your all from a dining room chair.

SCENE SEVEN

The lights go out.

You hear some sort of a thud. A muffled groan. The thick, wet slicing of something that reminds you of when your father used to take you hunting, which you're trying really hard not to think about. Your mind travels back to the knives in the block, and how stupid you were not to grab one at the time. Maybe you would be able to defend yourself—defend your boyfriend.

Was this person already in the house when they first spoke to you? Are your roommates even at the bar? Will they come home and find your body, gutted on the floor after all of this? Will your boyfriend get away? He's strong, he might be able to fight them off if he can pause and think for a moment. The odds of that last part are low, but we'll see.

There are too many thoughts going through your head to properly keep track of, so you pull yourself back to the present.

Back to the darkness of the living room, and the heat between your legs.

You're really trying not to think about how pleased the voice sounded when you did exactly as you were told. No matter how close the knife was to your boyfriend's throat or whatever. The threat didn't matter.

You did.

You're also definitely not thinking about those two words, and how just the sound of them caused something electric to light up inside of you.

Good girl.

You are good, aren't you? You do exactly as you're told, when you're told. You push your legs together, desperate for more of that friction from before. A small groan escapes your lips, and, lost in the moment, you forget that there's a person on the other end of the line.

"Enjoying yourself?"

The voice pulls you out of it, and your legs fall apart again.

"No, no," the voice continues, "don't stop on my account. If you're having fun, by all means, keep having fun."

But you don't want to do that anymore.

You feel squirmy and wrong, knowing that someone else is watching you—listening to you. What you're doing isn't right, you know it isn't right.

God, if anyone else was in your position, they would have called the police by now, wouldn't they?

Not you.

You're a good girl.

"Now, when the lights come back on, you can't make a sound, okay?" The voice sounds like it's attempting to reassure you, but also trying to stifle laughter at the same time. There's more rustling, like the sounds from the very first time you spoke.

"Okay," you whisper. "You didn't hurt him, did you?" You ask, in a vain attempt to gain some sort of truth from the voice on the other side. "You said you wouldn't."

You don't know if they'll even tell you the truth. You can hope for the best, but who knows, right?

"Just don't scream."

The room floods with light.

SCENE EIGHT

You scream even though the voice told you not to. It's hard to do anything else at the sight of it all.

Your boyfriend is out in the yard. Carved up like a deer for skinning.

His intestines are outside now, which is something you've seen plenty of times on a screen, but never in real life. You didn't think it would look quite so...red.

There's blood everywhere—so much blood, you didn't think a single person held that much blood. You know, of course, that the human body contains just over five liters, and your boyfriend is probably closer to six. You can conceptualize the idea of a liter, but you have no metric for understanding just how much that can be.

But now there it is. Most of his blood, close to all of it, if you had to guess.

All over your yard.

Dripping into your pool.

Spilling in circular patterns across the concrete, in a way that would surely stain.

You scream and you scream and you scream, and it is such a beautiful sound.

"You said you wouldn't!" You sob into the phone, your pretty makeup getting smudged by even prettier tears.

"Ohh," the voice chides, "I thought I told you not to do that."

Breath catching again, you stutter out an apology. It feels pointless now that your boyfriend is little more than ground beef, anything could happen.

"I'm sorry," you choke through tears, snot leaking out of your nose and down your lips.

"Too late."

The masked person isn't even there anymore, you realize. Your heart stutters out of beat, and your stomach tightens in a way that you don't particularly enjoy. Alongside that, the heat between your legs grows, which makes an uneasy nausea creep up your throat. A disgust with yourself. Is this *hot* to you?

Not your boyfriend, whose viscera is still sliding out from between cut flesh, but the tension. The chase. Not knowing who's under the mask, and the uncertainty of when they'll appear next. You have the phone, of course, but you don't really know. And they could do whatever the fuck they wanted to you.

That makes you wet, doesn't it?

It's almost like you want the voice to appear. You want the person behind the mask to wrap their hand around your pretty little throat and *squeeze*.

"Where'd you go?" You ask into the phone.

You can't tear your eyes away from him.

If you could, you might see the figure behind you, and it might give you some sort of advantage. But no, you're wrapped up in grief and arousal, and a confusing mix of self-hatred and something much, much deeper.

Before you can react, you get exactly what you wanted.

A hand around your throat, forcing you down into the chair once more. And then another hand, spreading your legs and forcing its way to your clit. And then a knife, held carefully against your throat, maybe the very same one you almost grabbed for yourself just moments ago.

And then a voice, whispering easily, "*Behave.*"

CLIMAX

You can't help yourself.

Your hips roll against the hand pressing your clit. The cool metal of the knife reminds you all too quickly that it is probably best you remain still.

The phone slides out of your hand, falling to the floor. It doesn't matter anymore. You got what you wanted. The figure, the voice, whatever this person is—they're here.

They're touching you.

And god, you love it.

"This is what you want, isn't it?" The same voice from the phone, tinny and false, crackles into your ear. "You didn't want your stupid boyfriend, you just wanted this."

You nod, letting your own desires betray any sort of loyalty you might've had to the dead man outside. It isn't even self-preservation at this point—it's genuine need.

"Good girl." There's a smile to the voice, though you can't see anything going on behind the mask.

A finger slips inside of you, and you moan, letting your head fall back again. Your movement is too quick, though, and the knife slides home, cutting a gash against the side of your neck that will probably need stitches.

No main arteries were cut though, so you aren't in any real danger.

Yet.

Still, you curse, and try to refrain from any intense physical-reaction.

"Don't move." It's a warning. Maybe a threat. You hold still—completely, perfectly still.

The finger curls upwards inside you, reaching a place that causes your eyes to roll back, and another low, desperate groan to pull from your throat.

The voice laughs, and another finger finds its way inside of you, pumping gently.

"Say that you want it," the voice instructs.

"I want it." You can't do anything but obey at this point.

You are good, after all.

You behave.

"What do you want?" The voice asks, as the knife gets pulled across your throat again, little bursts of pain left in its trail.

"I want you to fuck me."

There is no response. Just movement. Action.

The hand inside of you curls again and you gasp as the pace quickens, faster and harder than you fucked yourself earlier, giving you exactly what you wanted. Exactly what you asked for.

You peak far too quickly, much sooner than you would have liked, and you feel a hand clamp over your mouth as you start to scream. But you can't help yourself. Your eyes roll back, and your body is electric, alight with a mix of pain, pleasure, and so many other feelings you can't even begin to name.

Much like the first time, your whole body tenses. You feel the knife cut into your shoulder–deep. A punishment for moving. The pain of the wound mixes with the aftershock of the orgasm, and your vision goes black, stars and spots filling where there once was light.

The knife pulls away from your shoulder, and by the time you feel the stained slick of your own blood against your stomach, it's too late.

CURTAIN CALL

The knife feels good this time. You don't know if you can't feel the pain, or maybe there just isn't any, anymore. It slides home, finding a comfortable place in your abdomen. Not too deep. You're okay.

The plan—someone else's plan, not your own—is going exactly how they wanted it to, and the person behind the mask, the voice behind the phone, they all watch and listen as you moan and squirm when the blade slides home.

The figure pulls it out of you—a noticeable absence, a distinct lack of penetration—and then slams it inside of you again, letting the pure violence of the act take over. Your vision blurs, and suddenly, things feel a little too real.

It was never a game, you know that much. There was genuine terror, you felt real fear for your life. Your boyfriend is outside, dead on concrete, and, even though he was an asshole, he didn't really deserve that, did he?

But you had fun.

You can't deny that much.

You enjoyed yourself, *you sick fuck*, and you'd let them do it all again.

The knife pulls in and out of you, and you watch beautiful blooms of crimson pour from your stomach and chest, pools of liquid spilling out onto the floor, where it will definitely stain the carpet.

Back in the kitchen, the smoke alarm goes off–the QuickPop forgotten on the counter. Your roommates are sure to bitch and complain about it before they find your body.

You scream again, but that's okay.

No one told you not to.

DORI LUMPKIN

"GOOD SUFFERING"

A killer toes the line between gory past and hopeful present when she falls for a co-counselor at their summer camp; a high school girl recounts what really happened the night she murdered her best friend; the final two survivors of a doomed research expedition spend their final moments together. Dori Lumpkin's debut short story collection, GOOD SUFFERING, is an erotic love letter to classic horror movies in which Dori examines the thin line between arousal, exploitation, and terror.

Dori Lumpkin is a queer writer and storytelling enthusiast from South Alabama. Their work has appeared in *The Deeps*, *Demons & Death Drops*, and many other places. They love all things horror and weird, and strive to make fiction writing a more inclusive place.

You can find them at the handle @whimsyqueen on most social media websites, or visit their website:

https://dorilumpkin.carrd.co/

Made in the USA
Middletown, DE
02 September 2024

60234175R00097